"But we're here now and we're alone."

"That we are," she said, knowing the exact moment his lips would touch hers.

From the center of the fountain just a few feet away, ten-foot jets of water spouted and fell in a lighted display. Sam's lips touched hers and her eyes fluttered shut. The sound of rushing water echoed in the distance but all she could think about was the soft touch of his lips on hers, the warmth of his tongue slipping past her teeth and moving seductively into her mouth.

Wrapping her arms around his neck and tilting her head for better access she took him in, moaning as he sucked her tongue with deep hungry strokes, sinking closer into his embrace as he masterfully seduced her with his mouth.

Never before had she been kissed like this. Surely this must be a dream. Either that or it was forbidden. Nothing that tasted this good, felt this right, could be good for her. Hadn't she already learned that lesson?

D1005548

Books by A.C. Arthur

Kimani Romance

Love Me Like No Other
A Cinderella Affair
Guarding His Body
Second Chance, Baby
Defying Desire
Full House Seduction
Summer Heat

A.C. ARTHUR

was born and raised in Baltimore, Maryland, where she currently resides with her husband and three children. An active imagination and a love for reading encouraged her to begin writing in high school and she hasn't stopped since.

Determined to bring a new edge to romance, she continues to develop intriguing plots, racy characters and fresh dialogue—thus keeping readers on their toes! Visit her Web site at www.acarthur.net.

Summer
HEAT

A.C. Arthur

To Kimberly L. Arthur
Thanks for the candid words of inspiration.

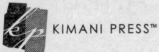

KIMANI PRESS™

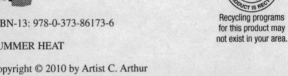

ISBN-13: 978-0-373-86173-6

Recycling programs
for this product may
not exist in your area.

SUMMER HEAT

www.kimanipress.com

Printed in U.S.A.

Dear Reader,

Welcome to the art world and to the legacy of the beautiful and talented Lakefields of Manhattan. Once again I have given you a family of strong, independent and successful adults—this time in the form of three intriguing sisters—Monica, Karena and Deena.

When I envisioned the perfect woman for Sam Desdune I knew she would have to be multi-dimensional. Sam would want a woman who was independent and sexy, yet compassionate and loving. I also knew that bringing Sam and Karena together was going to take something really special, so I went out on a limb with a beautiful Brazilian beach, an endearing Great Dane and the tried and true tale of *Romeo and Juliet*.

I hope you enjoy this first look into the Lakefields and stay tuned for more!

As always, I would love to hear from you. I can be contacted at acarthur22@yahoo.com.

Happy reading!

A.C. Arthur

Prologue

Karena Lakefield took her seat on the plane and immediately buckled her seat belt, just as she did when getting into a car. It was just one of those things she was anal about. Actually, if her sisters were telling it, they'd say she was anal about just about everything. She, however, liked to think of it as having an orderly life—everything in its place and all that.

That's how she managed her business dealings, her family issues and her personal life—otherwise, she would have checked into the sanitarium by now.

She was just about to reach into her bag and pull out her laptop when the seat beside her was taken.

"Hello, again," Sam Desdune said with an easy smile that once again had Karena's toes warming.

"Well, hello to you. I didn't know we were booked on the same flight."

"Neither did I. Originally I was going to stay another day just to make sure that things went smoothly with Luther's extradition. But Brock assured me that he'd go down to the police station to personally see the man off." With that, Sam had packed his overnight bag and headed for the airport, hoping to find a flight leaving for New York sooner rather than later. And lady luck seemed to be on his side—in more ways than one, he noted as he looked into the cheerfully pretty face of Karena Lakefield.

They'd officially met last night at dinner, the one where Brock announced that Noelle would be moving to the East Coast with him—and Jade nearly fell out of her chair. The memory had Sam chuckling. He'd known Trent Donovan for almost ten years. He'd shared some of the Donovan family dinners and enjoyed them immensely, but none as much as last night's.

The lady with the coal-black hair styled in a short spiky do and dark, seductive eyes was the cause for that.

She was one of the Lakefields of Manhattan. The minute Noelle had said her name, he'd made the connection. The Lakefields ran the most exclusive and affluent African-American-owned art galleries in the United States. And while his brother-in-law, Lorenzo Bennett, had just recently opened his own gallery, Renny had nothing on the Lakefields' status in the art world.

That's exactly the impression Karena gave him: refined, delicate, priceless—a piece of art worth buying for whatever price was asked.

"Good. I'm glad that whole episode is over. I feel so bad for Noelle and all that she's been through."

"Yeah, but she's got Brock now, so I'm sure she'll be well taken care of from here on out."

"Humph, must be nice," she said with a frown then looked out the window.

The plane was just about to take off when Karena's cell phone chimed. She cursed and answered it quickly, looking around to make sure none of the flight attendants noticed that she hadn't turned it off as they'd asked.

"Hello?" she whispered.

"What? Monica, I'm on the plane. Can this wait until I get home? No, I don't leave again for another two weeks.

"It'll be fine if we wait, Monica. Yes. I know." She rolled her eyes skyward and sucked in a breath as the plane lifted from the ground. The worst parts of flying were takeoff and landing, in her book.

"I know, Monica. Look, I'm hanging up. I'll call you when I get home.

"Okay," she sighed. "I'll call you when we land."

"Trouble on the home front?" Sam asked when she'd snapped the phone closed, turned it off and stuffed it into her purse.

"Not exactly. My older sister, Monica, is a slave driver."

"Really?"

"Yeah, she manages our family gallery in Manhattan while I do all the buying and supervise the sales division."

"I see, a family business. I know all about those."

"Are you in a family business?"

"Nah, I'm one of the apples that fell far from the tree," he chuckled. "My family owns restaurants up and down the eastern seaboard. But at my P.I. firm I employ mostly family members. My twin sister and Trent's cousin to name a few."

"That's right, you and Trent are good friends. Well, I'll tell you, people are constantly telling me to get a life, but Monica is the one who needs to take a chill pill," Karena said with a grin.

"Really? That's interesting," Sam said thoughtfully.

"How so?"

"Is Monica involved with anyone right now?"

"No. Didn't you hear when I said she was a workaholic? The only way she could be involved is if she's sneaking a man into the gallery after hours, because I swear that girl sleeps there."

"I think I know somebody who would get along famously with her."

Karena frowned. "I don't usually do the matchmaking thing," she began. "But tell me about him anyway." She was smiling and turning sideways to look at him.

"He's my brother-in-law's older brother. His name is Alexander Bennett, but we just call him Alex. I don't think he ever peels himself away from his desk either."

So as the plane soared higher into the clouds, Sam and Karena talked about Alex and Monica, then about their jobs and finally about themselves. By the time the plane landed, they'd exchanged all contact information with a promise to call when they had some free time.

A promise Sam happily planned to keep.

September—Gramercy II Grand Opening, Maryland

"You never called," Sam whispered over her shoulder.

Karena turned, the smile spreading across her face, slowly but impulsively and probably giving away how happy she was to see him. "Neither did you."

"Guilty," he said, lifting her hand to his lips and kissing its back. "Forgive me?"

She was still smiling, feeling like a high-school girl on her prom night. "No big deal." Karena pulled her hand from his, because this was getting too weird.

Sure, she'd met Sam Desdune last month when she'd come to check on her best friend, Noelle. And yes, he was handsome, easy to talk to and had made her flight back to New York very pleasant. But it wasn't as though he was a long-distance boyfriend—or even a long-distance friend, for that matter.

He lived in Connecticut and she in Manhattan. They weren't that far away, and yet neither had tried to contact the other after their first meeting. Perhaps the tiny flutters she'd felt while sitting next to him on the plane were really nothing.

"So what do you think?" Sam asked, his gaze moving around the room of the Gramercy II, the sister casino/resort owned by Lincoln Donovan of the Las Vegas Donovans and run by Noelle Vincent, Karena's best friend and Linc's sister-in-law.

"It's fabulous," she answered without hesitation. "But then if Noelle had her hand in it, I wouldn't expect anything less."

Sam was nodding in agreement. "Yeah, it turned out really well. Linc's thrilled."

"That's wonderful. I know Noelle really wanted to impress him."

"Well, I'd say she did that and then some."

Conversation tapered off as they each looked around the room, then as if it were planned, Sam touched a hand to her elbow and escorted her out of the main casino room. They walked along the high-ceilinged corridor with its copper-toned fountain running down one side and lighted walkway along the plush sage-green carpet.

The atmosphere was calming and relaxing, which seemed a bit strange for a casino. Yet it fit this small water community, the splash of decadence and bling mixing seamlessly with the quiet ambiance, creating a unique feel that was sure to attract a lot of customers.

Karena felt the relaxation but instinctively fought it. She had so much work to do when she returned to the city, which was why instead of taking Noelle's offer to stay at the house she shared with Brock Remington, her boyfriend and Linc Donovan's cousin, Karena opted to stay here at the Gramercy II for the night and take a flight out first thing in the morning.

Why she couldn't relax enough to take a vacation was beyond her. No, actually it wasn't. It was her choice, her goals in life, the limitations she set for herself, all her choice, her doing, her need.

Coming to another airy space centered by a larger fountain, this one with copper railings to keep guests from venturing too close to the water display that was presented every other hour, she and Sam stopped.

"It's nice here," she said, tired of the endless quiet between them. It felt odd to be with this man and not talk, because he was so easy to communicate with, unlike other men who would have probably been pawing all over her by now. Maybe Sam wasn't interested in her in that way. And why should she care?

"It's quieter here. There were too many people in the other room. I didn't want any distractions," he said seriously.

His hand was still on her elbow as they faced each other. "You're at a casino/resort opening, how could you not want to be in the casino?"

"I'm here to support a friend," he said, speaking of his best friend and business partner, Trent Donovan. "The Donovans are like extended family to me, so it's great to see them taking on another successful venture."

"All the more reason you would want to be out there."

"Nah," he said, taking a step closer to her and lifting his other hand to touch her cheek. "Not when I can take advantage of being alone with you."

Okay, so she wasn't crazy. The fizzle of attraction she'd felt when they'd met last month hadn't been a fluke. And it was back, alive and sparkling as they stood, feeling tiny drops of mist as the water show prepared to begin.

"You could have been alone with me before if you'd called," she said, surprising herself with her boldness. Being with a man wasn't new to Karena, but she wasn't the flowers, romance and courting type. Because of her hectic lifestyle and those endless limitations she put on herself, her encounters with the opposite sex needed to be quick and efficient. So if there was something brewing between her and Sam Desdune, maybe it was best they act on it quickly and keep it moving.

"I could and should have. But we're here now and we're alone."

"That we are," she said, knowing the exact moment his lips would touch hers.

From the center of the fountain just a few feet away, ten-foot jets of water spewed and fell in a lighted display. Sam's lips touched hers and her eyes fluttered shut. The sound of rushing water echoed in the distance, but all she could think about was the soft touch of his lips on hers, the warmth of his tongue slipping past her teeth and moving seductively into her mouth.

Wrapping her arms around his neck and tilting her head for better access, she took him in, moaning as he sucked her tongue with deep hungry strokes, sinking closer into his embrace as he masterfully seduced her with his mouth.

Never before had she been kissed like this. Surely this must be a dream. Either that or it was forbidden. Nothing that tasted this good, felt this right, could be good for her. Hadn't she already learned that lesson?

Chapter 1

October—Lakefield Galleries, New York City

"Stolen? That's impossible!" Karena slammed her palms flat on her desk then stood.

Dropping down into the paisley-patterned guest chair across from her was her oldest sister and biggest critic, Monica Lakefield. Monica was the manager of Lakefield Galleries, their family-owned and for the most part family-run art gallery in Manhattan.

In addition to being extremely intelligent Monica was as ambitious, cutthroat and relentless as any Brooks Brothers suit-wearing man in corporate America—a fact she relished.

Karena was two years younger than Monica, having celebrated her thirtieth birthday six months ago. She considered herself ambitious as well, a trait clearly inherited from their domineering father, Paul. But she wasn't as hard as Monica, not as rigid and stern when it came to business—or everything else for that matter.

"It's right there in black and white," Monica was saying as she tossed a manila folder onto Karena's desk. Sighing heavily, Karena moved to pick up the folder. No way this was happening to her. She'd had a rough enough time trying to sleep last night due to dreams that she definitely should not be having. And now this. It was barely ten in the morning and Monica was delivering this disastrous news.

"Jacques did the appraisal, just like he always does. He checked with the ASA and the ADAA. It's either a fake or it's stolen. He has a few more tests to run, but odds are it's stolen."

Karena's fingers shook slightly as she leafed through the pages. Sure enough, there were three reports: one from Jacques, one from the Appraisers Association of America and the final one from the Art Dealers Association of America. Hearing Monica sum up the reports in front of her in such cold and succinct language had her heart pounding, the sound throbbing in her ears.

"I met with him personally. We had breakfast on the terrace in Pirata. He even showed me the cliffs where he liked to paint at dawn."

"Oh, please. Karena, he played you like a prized violin. He didn't paint that picture. He's not Leandro."

"There's a mistake. There's got to be some mistake," she insisted. Because if there wasn't, then her sister was right. She'd been played by the quietly handsome man who stood six feet tall with somber brown eyes and nut-brown skin.

His heavily accented voice had been a little hard for her to understand, but it didn't matter once he showed her the first painting. Immediately she'd fallen in love with the colors, the tone, the simplicity of the piece. She'd had to have it. Lakefield Galleries had to have it.

And now they did. A stolen portrait that could totally destroy the reputation they'd spent years building.

"Did you get any form of identification? I mean, damn, what made you believe it was even him? For more than a year he's been unreachable, his paintings appearing only in small galleries spread out over the world. Not even his agent has ever met him in person." Monica waved a hand as she spoke, her signature long painted nails catching bits of the fluorescent lighting.

"I didn't card him, Monica. That's not normally how I do business. And remember, he called me." The call had come just as Karena had returned from Maryland, where she'd been attending the grand opening of the Gramercy II, the casino her best friend, Noelle Vincent, and her boyfriend, Brock Remington, had built.

The resort was the East Coast version of one of Las Vegas's hottest casinos owned by Lincoln Donovan, of the illustrious Donovan clan. It was through Linc that Karena had met Noelle and forged one of the closest friendships she'd ever had.

The moment she'd stepped off the plane from Maryland and turned on her cell phone, it rang. On the other end, calling all the way from Pirata, a medium-size town in Brazil, was Leandro, the reclusive oil-painting artist now blowing up in the art world. The minute he'd said his name, she'd been ready to board another plane to visit him.

In less than a week she'd been in Brazil, soaking up the gorgeous scenery and sitting across from the man who was about to give her the biggest sale of her art-buying career.

Had he lied to her?

"Maybe you need a lesson in how to do business?"

Both Monica and Karena stilled at the sound of his voice. He'd opened the door and walked right into her office, no announcement from her secretary needed. After all, he owned Lakefield Galleries and the Lakefield Foundation.

"If it's truly stolen, where did it come from? Because right now there's no proof that the man I met with wasn't Leandro," Karena said, trying like hell to hide the nervousness being in the same room as her father inevitably brought.

He was angry. No, not quite so, more like annoyed. His broad body wore a designer suit as if Ralph Lauren himself had come to the mansion and cut the material around him. His thick wavy hair hadn't started to fall out, which was more and more common for men over fifty-five these days. Instead, Paul Lakefield's hair had turned a sparkling gray, taking him from handsome to distinguished in the past five years. His dark eyes were what threw off the otherwise handsome package. Those eyes always seemed to pin Karena with accusation.

Her birth wasn't a mistake, not entirely, just her sex. Her entire life her father had made no secret of the fact that he'd wanted a son. Proving that there were some things Paul Lakefield could not control, the good Lord blessed him with three daughters instead.

"How did you ship the painting?" her father asked, slipping his hands into his pant pockets.

"Like I always do, Federal Express International, with insurance. I packaged it myself before it left the estate where we stayed. I labeled the box and spoke to the carrier. From that point on anything could have happened."

Monica was already shaking her head. "Jacques thinks it's one of the paintings stolen from members of the royal family."

Karena's head ached. She wanted to rub her temples but refrained from showing any sign of weakness in front of her father. And her sister, for that matter. Neither of them would understand what she was going through. Hell, she doubted she understood it herself.

"There's a royal family in Brazil?" Paul asked.

"A prince, I think," Monica said and reached for the folder, which Karena quickly closed and gripped tightly.

"Great," Paul huffed. "Now they'll think the Lakefields are thieves."

"I doubt they know who the Lakefields are all the way in Brazil," Monica stated quietly, her eyes sweeping to Karena.

"Exactly my point. Now their first impression of us will be that we stole from them."

Karena felt sick. Her stomach quivered and her head throbbed so hard she could feel the vibration throughout her entire body. This room was too small for all three of them. In fact, sometimes she thought the whole world was too small for her and her family.

"I'll take care of it," she snapped and was already moving toward the door.

"Let me help, Karena. This is our name on the line," Monica stated coolly.

"No, it's my buy, I'll handle it."

"Yes. You handle it, and do it fast before word gets out," Paul said solemnly.

Karena opened her mouth to speak then clapped her lips shut.

Three things were drilled into her and her sisters as they grew up in the Lakefield household: Loyalty. Honesty. Respect.

Only her upbringing held the words she'd longed to say to her father at bay, while the terrible fear that she'd truly messed up guided her quick steps.

Samuel Desdune fell back on the ground laughing as his two-year-old blue Great Dane tackled him to the ground, red ball hanging from his mouth.

Fall was just creeping up on the quiet Greenwich, Connecticut, neighborhood he lived in, delivering a crisp morning breeze in its wake. The trees and shrubs surrounding Sam's waterfront home were just beginning to show signs of color change, and Romeo was enjoying his morning exercise.

It had been a year since Sam had adopted Romeo from National Great Dane Rescue after Romeo's battle with kidney failure. Initially Romeo had a fear of all men except Sam, which made it quite difficult when Sam's older brother, Cole, or his father, Lucien, came for a visit. But then his sister Lynn had brought her four-year-old son, Jeremy, over and Romeo's attitude toward the male gender had changed.

Rolling Romeo off him, Sam retrieved the ball from the dog's mouth, got to his feet and tossed it the length of the yard once more. Romeo, with his shiny blue-gray coat and long legs, practically leaped across the grass to retrieve it.

Oh, the joys of being his own boss. D&D Investigations was in its sixth month of business. For two years prior Sam hadn't had a partner, but after the biggest case of his new career so far—tracking and capturing the man who stalked and terrorized the Bennett family—he'd decided a partner would be nice. For that he'd called on his old friend, Trent Donovan, an ex-Navy SEAL with instincts Sam trusted and a kick-ass attitude he admired even though it still scared him a bit.

Trent ran the West Coast location while Sam concentrated on the East Coast cases. Right now they were handling the surveillance of a cheating husband and the disappearance of a four-year-old girl. For both cases, his twin sister, Sabrina, and Trent's cousin Bailey could hold down the fort. Bree, the nickname he would always use for his twin, no matter who she married or how many kids she had, was a former Marine. She could hold her own, as she'd shown without a doubt when she'd chased and injured the stalker who was about to shoot her husband, Lorenzo Bennett.

Bailey Donovan was, for lack of a better term, a loose cannon. She was antsy and reckless and itching for some action. That's why Trent had sent her to Sam, because he didn't have time to babysit her now that he was married and about to become a father.

For now, however, the missing-child case was making good use of Bailey's excess energy as she followed lead after lead in the hopes of finding the child before Christmas.

Romeo was back, his natural ears flapping against the breeze as he returned the ball once more. "Good boy," Sam was saying as the cell phone at his hip began to ring.

"Desdune," he said answering after the second ring.

"Hi, I hope you remember me. This is Karena Lake-field."

The red ball fell out of Sam's hand as Romeo with his large, sometimes awkward body danced around Sam demanding attention.

Of course he remembered her. The petite, brown-skinned beauty with intriguing eyes and tight body he'd met while in Maryland helping Trent with a family problem. How could he forget her?

"Hi, Karena," he said cheerfully. "It's nice to hear from you."

They'd exchanged phone numbers on the plane ride back from Maryland in August and then saw each other again briefly at the opening of the Gramercy II in early September.

No. Sam hadn't forgotten. She'd felt like sunshine in his arms, then dripped like molten lava when he'd kissed her. He'd wanted to take her up to one of the rooms at the Gramercy II, thought she wanted the same. Then she'd pulled away, left him standing, getting wet in front of the water show, and he hadn't spoken to her again.

Until now.

"I need your help," she said, her voice sounding less

like the sexy timbre he remembered and just on this side of desperate.

"What's wrong?"

"I'm in trouble," she sighed. "Big trouble."

Chapter 2

Sam couldn't say he was happy about driving into Manhattan on a day he'd planned to spend rolling around in the yard with Romeo.

And he couldn't say that he liked the tone of Karena's voice as she asked for help.

What he could say was that he was looking forward to seeing her again. As his body heated thinking about her in the tight jeans and even tighter T-shirt she'd worn on the plane ride they'd shared, he admitted he was *really* looking forward to seeing her.

Talking to her on the two occasions he'd seen her had been like a breath of fresh air. While she tended to talk too much about her job, as if there was nothing more interesting in the world to her, Sam got the impression she was witty and adventurous, even if she didn't know it herself. From Noelle he'd learned that she was the middle child of three daughters, born into a very wealthy family now making their name in the art world. Upon returning from his first trip to Maryland he'd run a check on Karena's father, Paul Lakefield, and came up with a brief family history.

The Lakefields' wealth stemmed all the way back to California's historic Gold Rush in 1848, when a slave named Celia Smith was taken by her master's cousin from Virginia across the country. George Lakefield had instantly fallen for his cousin's housemaid on a visit to Virginia, and before he'd left he'd had Celia in his bed. Upon agreement with his cousin, George took ownership of Celia and headed west to take up with the other panhandlers in search of gold.

That search led to George Lakefield's first taste of fortune. In 1863, when President Lincoln declared the freedom of all slaves, Celia Smith had stayed by George's side, and in the years ahead gave birth to four sons and one daughter. Two of the Lakefield sons moved on to Texas, where they struck oil, while the other two ventured into the steel business. The daughter married and stayed in California, where her descendents now ran the successful Genoa Winery.

It was Paul's great-grandfather, Mathias Lakefield, who took Lakefield Steel to its victorious holdings, leaving a legacy for Paul and his two brothers to follow.

A very impressive history, Sam remembered thinking as he read, leading to more intrigue about Karena. The first time he'd met her, she'd seemed worried about Noelle and the idiotic ex-boyfriend of Noelle's Sam had helped Trent and the other Donovan brothers capture. But once that situation was settled and Sam talked to her on the plane, he'd noticed something else about her: she was totally dedicated to her job and her family.

Did that sound familiar?

Of course it did. There was nothing—and Sam readily emphasized the word *nothing*—that he wouldn't do for his family. Born and raised in Louisiana, Lucien and Marie

Desdune were Creole. That was the name given to persons of various racial mixes who were descended from the colonial French and Spanish settlers of Louisiana and from African-Americans and Native Americans.

The Desdunes were a cultivated mixture of French and African-American ancestry. As such, twenty years ago Lucien had opened his self-named Creole-and-Cajun restaurant in New Orleans. Since that time, Lucien's had expanded to four popular restaurants along the eastern seaboard. Unfortunately, Lucien's children hadn't all gone into the same line of work. Sam's oldest sister, Lynn, was a domestic law attorney, while Bree had gone the military route before settling into security and now private investigation with Sam. Cole, the second oldest, was the only one who'd taken to his father's love of cooking, now working as an executive chef and manager of Lucien's in New York. To be closer to their children, who all seemed to move from Louisiana once they'd graduated high school, Lucien and Marie also lived in Connecticut.

So yes, Sam knew a little bit about being loyal to his family, to a certain extent. In talking with Karena on those previous occasions, Sam had immediately sensed she had problems drawing the line between her family's expectations and her own desires.

The sound of blaring horns and the stop and go of traffic reminded Sam of how much he hated coming into the city. Still, he'd kept his composure even when one of those notorious cab drivers cut him off. It was that control that had gained him his reputation of being levelheaded and the best person to have around in high-pressure situations.

He'd almost smiled as he remembered finding out that Bree had been assaulted. At that point, Sam recalled, he lost that reputed composure, wanted to lace his fingers around the neck of Harold Richmond, the now-jailed former colonel from the United States Marine Corps. The only other time Sam had lost his cool was when his older sister Lynn's ex-husband had been stupid enough to slash her tires and kick her door in before packing and leaving his wife and young son for good.

He sighed, realizing he definitely knew about loving one's family.

The address Karena had given him was coming up just ahead, and Sam made one last maneuver through busy Manhattan traffic before pulling into the narrow garage opening. Stopping again, he retrieved the parking ticket, tucked it into his windshield and proceeded through the rounding maze until he found a spot.

Ten minutes later he watched as the elevator doors opened to the seventh floor. Stepping off the elevator onto the dark marble floor, he walked the few steps to the glass doors with *Lakefield Galleries* in wide gold letters hanging above.

Inside those doors the floor was carpeted, a dusky gray color with cool black furniture and an even paler gray paint on the walls. Behind the reception area sat an Asian woman, her long hair dark as onyx, her eyes friendly as she turned to him.

"Good afternoon, welcome to Lakefield Galleries. How may I help you?"

Her voice echoed in the large space.

"Sam Desdune, here to see Karena Lakefield," he replied easily.

"Of course," she stood, coming around the desk to stand beside him. "Ms. Lakefield's expecting you. Follow me, please."

Sam surveyed more of his surroundings while walking behind the courteous receptionist.

No money had been spared in the building and maintaining of this gallery. As they'd rounded the corner to a long hallway, the walls turned to a crisp white. Pictures were hung at carefully measured intervals. Not a real fan of art that went beyond green pastures and lakes, he found himself pleasantly surprised by the abstract designs that carried a theme throughout the office space. He was wondering what the rest of the gallery looked like when the receptionist stopped in front of double black-lacquer doors, opening one and waving him inside.

"Thanks," he said before stepping inside. Behind him he heard the quiet click of the door being closed.

Although it was only a couple of feet away it sounded distant, and the memory of the receptionist's smile and friendly voice faded from his mind. The curiosity about the rest of the gallery also fell to the side as she stood from the high-backed leather chair she'd been sitting in and walked toward him.

This was the scene in movies where the music supervisors played an up-tempo track then let it pause. The camera captured his eyes then hers, panning out until her entire body was in view.

Petite didn't accurately describe her, although she was no more than five feet two or three inches without heels. It was the curves that made that word an understatement where she was concerned. The dip of a slender waist spanned to perfectly rounded hips, taking his gaze on a slow, heated ride down to toned legs covered only midway to her thigh, where the dress she wore abruptly stopped.

Nylons covered her legs, he sensed, although the sheer, silky caramel color could have been her bare skin. Classy, expensive and sexy black leather pumps sported heels so high their purpose could only be to tempt a man to distraction.

The song "Fire and Desire" by Rick James and Teena Marie immediately played in his head. Although he hadn't loved and left her, Karena Lakefield was definitely tempting him, positively heating a fire in him that he'd wondered if he'd ever experience again. Just as petite didn't accurately describe her, desire did not fully capture what he was feeling for her at this very moment.

"Hi, Sam. Thanks for coming so soon," she said, extending her hand to him.

Swallowing the thick ball of lust that had lodged itself so comfortably in his throat, Sam took her hand and knew exactly what Rick James had been singing about.

Taking her hand in his, Karena Lakefield had effectively turned on a fire in Sam that would be hell trying to put out.

Chapter 3

Sam cleared his throat and shook his head as if trying to rid his mind of something.

His hand gripped hers tightly and Karena lifted her free hand to his elbow. "Are you okay?" she asked, full of concern.

"Fine," he said, his voice breaking just slightly. "I'm fine. You said you were in trouble," he finished and released his grip.

"Yes," she said, still not sure if he was all right but resigned to getting down to the pressing matter at hand. "Something strange is going on and I wanted to see if you could help me."

Moving back to her chair, she sat then motioned for Sam to sit in the chair beside hers. They were in the west conference room, the smaller one on this floor but still large enough to hold fifty people. This was where they held press conferences or hosted small receptions.

Reaching out, she spread the papers and photos from the file she'd been reviewing all morning. After Monica's bombshell about the stolen painting, she'd wanted to read up on everything she had on the artist known as Leandro and compare it with the man she'd met in Brazil.

Sam sat, quickly looked down at the papers and touched a finger to one of the photos.

"It's called 'Awake,'" she informed him about the painting she thought she'd purchased from Leandro.

He nodded. "Because of the sun rising," he stated blandly.

"No," she touched the picture, tracing her finger along the line where the ocean met the simmering rays of the mounting sun. "Because it awakens the senses. It pulls you in from the moment you look at it. Whether you think of the coolness of the water against your skin or the scent of the tropical air blowing in the distance, you instantly become a part of the painting."

His fingers moved from the intense orange-and-crimson tone of the sun to stop just beside hers. Where she traced the water line, he did the same, until the tips of their fingers touched.

Karena felt a jolt to her system. A quick piercing sensation started at the exact point where he'd touched her and moved quickly throughout her body. Frowning, she moved her hand and picked up another sheet of paper.

"Two weeks ago I went to Brazil to meet an artist," she said, then recounted a brief history of Leandro. "He does oil paintings and has been on the scene for about two years now. His work is in high demand but extremely hard to come by. He doesn't do shows, no appearances, no interviews. All pieces are purchased directly from his agent and he usually remains anonymous."

"But you met him?" Sam inquired.

"He called me," she said, looking up at him.

He lifted a brow in question. "The reclusive artist called you? Why?"

A woman would kill for thick, even eyebrows such as his. His complexion was the color of honey fresh out of the jar. Eyes that were dark, yet warm, held her gaze steadily. He wore brown slacks and a lighter-shade short-sleeved shirt that fit his muscled chest precisely. It was still reasonably warm outside so a jacket wasn't really necessary. This fact afforded her the opportunity to see even more of his toned arms, ribboned with veins that showed his sheer strength.

Was her mouth watering?

Now it was her turn to clear her throat. "I...I don't know, really. And to tell the truth I was too excited to ask. It was the day we flew back from Maryland. He called before I left the airport. I booked another flight out the next evening and met with him on a Wednesday morning."

"He picked you up at the airport?"

He was staring at her intently, as though he could see into her mind and therefore really didn't need to ask her questions. Her pulse quickened and she flattened her palms on the table.

"No. I took a cab to the address he'd given me."

"To his house?"

"Yes." She blinked then attempted to focus more on her trip to Brazil than on the man sitting—now that she thought about it—too damned close to her. "No. Well, I guess it was his house. I didn't really ask."

"Did you stay with him? In this house, I mean. Did you stay there during your trip?"

Karena was sure these questions had something to do with the stolen pictures, but her mind kept wrapping around the slight edge in his voice, the intensity of his gaze as he waited for her answers.

"I stayed, yes. There was a cottage on the property and he said I could stay there."

Sam sat back in the chair, his tall, built form moving so that it swiveled to the side. Her view of him increased, as now she could see muscled thighs even through the loose-fitting pants he wore. He rested his elbows on the arms of the chair, then lifted one hand to rub his fingers along his chin. Except for a thin mustache his face was clean-shaven, giving him a neat, quiet allure.

"The house was big. Did it look like he had money or did he truly give the impression of a starving artist?"

What she saw looked too good. Sam was too attractive. Had he looked like this when she'd met him in Maryland? Or had the weeks since she'd seen him simply added to the days of her self-imposed celibacy, coloring her present perception of him?

"It was like a mansion or something. There was a lot of property."

"And just the one cottage where you stayed?"

"No, there were several cottages." Then shaking her head, she held up a hand and said, "Wait a minute. You're asking me about where I slept and how I got to his house. But none of this has anything to do with the fact that the appraiser's report says the painting was stolen. My question is how does an artist steal his own painting?"

He wanted to know where she'd slept. Had she been in this artist's—this man's—house, in a bedroom next to his or, heaven forbid, in his bed. It was insane, Sam knew without having to mentally kick himself with the thought. Karena wasn't his, and thinking of her with another man should not have his fists itching to punch someone. Looking at her should not be tugging on something primal, hungry, inside of him.

And yet…

"I'm trying to paint my own picture of sorts," he said,

giving her the best part of a smile he had to force. "This is a recluse, an up-until-now private person, who calls you out of the blue. He wants to what, sell you a portrait? Or does he want to meet you personally? Were you targeted for some reason?"

She was shaking her head, the diamond-stud earrings sparkling in her ears. Her short, sophisticated hairdo was neat and precise and sexy as hell. Sam usually enjoyed women with hair that he could run his fingers through, but on her that look would be too much, overwhelming the delicate beauty of her small facial features.

"This isn't about me. It's about the fact that I purchased a portrait that was obviously stolen."

"Nothing is obvious, Karena," he said honestly.

"So what are you saying?"

"I'm saying that you have a history of this guy. He doesn't talk to anyone, doesn't do showings, doesn't seem to want anyone to know who he is or where he is. His work is good and is in high demand. So why all the secrecy? Then he calls you. Of all the art galleries in all the world he picks you and the Lakefield Galleries. Why?"

"Because we're good," she said, apparently ruffled by his words.

He nodded. "I'm not disputing that fact. I'm just pointing out a few things. How did he know you'd come if he called? Had you been trying to find him?"

"No. Actually, I hadn't. I knew his history. Once, earlier last year I contacted his agent about a showing, but I assured her that he wasn't required to show up."

"Didn't his phone call strike you as weird?"

"Yes." Now that she thought about it, it had.

"He called your cell phone. How many people have that number? Do you have a separate cell phone for business and personal use?"

"No. I have one phone, but I have two numbers. Kind of like an extension within the phone."

"So he called which extension? Business or personal?"

She thought for a minute, remembered the distinctive ringtones she'd programmed to tell her which type of call was incoming. And she sighed. "He called the personal number."

"You think this man targeted my company for some reason?" Paul Lakefield asked Sam fifteen minutes later when he and Monica Lakefield had joined him and Karena in the conference room.

Paul Lakefield was tall, brooding and stern, all characteristics Sam could respect. He was also judgmental. The tone of his voice, the way in which he'd looked at Sam the moment he'd entered the conference room, said he was neither impressed nor thrilled that Sam was here. Even when Karena had introduced him as being a business partner of Trent Donovan's, one of the Donovans renowned for their own success in business as well as their philanthropy.

Not that Sam cared. His business was steadily building its own credibility and reputation, and he didn't need Paul Lakefield's approval. He was here only because Karena had called him.

"I'm saying that I don't believe it was coincidence that he called Karena offering not only to sell her a painting but to also meet her in person."

"Maybe he's making a move on behalf of his career. Coming out of hiding to further build on his name," Karena said, hope tinting her voice.

"Or maybe it was a setup all along."

This was from Monica, Karena's sister. Her older sister, he surmised from the impatient look she gave Karena.

Monica was the polar opposite of Karena in the looks

department. She was taller for one, probably around five feet eight or nine inches, her frame svelte and sophisticated. Her clothes matched her personality, designer business suit with starched white blouse and heels that put her directly at eye level with him. She was cool, professional and determined to prove she was as good as any man. Sam had seen her type before.

She was a beautiful woman, there was no doubt about that. Her complexion was a few shades lighter than Karena's, her features stronger, more defined. Her hair was pulled back into a tight bun that probably only added to her uptight attitude. All in all, if Sam had his choice of whom he'd like to be trapped on a deserted island with, Karena won, hands down.

Sam was a detail man. He paid attention to everything around him, even the things that people themselves didn't realize they were doing.

Karena was sitting in the exact spot she'd been in before her father and sister arrived, only now she wasn't as talkative or as assertive in her position. Monica had taken a seat beside her, but it was clear she was on her father's side. Or was she playing the mediator between Karena and Paul?

"This should never have happened. You should have checked things out before going down there."

"Checked things out how, Daddy? Should I have had the number he called from traced? Asked him to send me his photo identification and Social Security card?" She sighed heavily and began gathering the papers from the table. "I've hired Sam to look into this. Until then, the picture stays in our warehouse. I mean, Jacques hasn't even produced a name of the alleged true owners of the portrait. And I haven't seen an insurance claim for the stolen property."

Standing, she lifted the folder in her hands, took a deep breath and looked at her father once more. "I got us into this and I'll make sure we get out of it. Just like I told you earlier this morning."

In that moment Sam saw her strength, her dedication not only to her job but to her family. And when her father hadn't responded but only looked at her solemnly, Sam saw something else. Hurt.

"This is my company, Karena. I'm just trying to make sure we all keep our dealings aboveboard," Paul offered as if he'd seen that flash of pain in his daughter's eyes, as well.

"With all due respect, Daddy, the gallery is my domain," Monica offered. "I'm the manager and Jacques reports directly to me. So I'll keep a close eye on this and fill you in as the need arises."

Paul's gaze moved from one daughter to the other. "The need has already arisen. I want to know every development in this matter. If you're going to investigate, know that we'll pay top dollar for priority as well as privacy," he said to Sam.

"That's not required. I know how to do my job." That was something Paul hadn't expected him to say, Sam was sure. But he'd been more than a little concerned with the way Paul Lakefield handled his daughters. It was as if they had positions within his company but he was still in control, no matter what. His trust in them was nonexistent, and Sam was willing to bet the sisters knew this and detested their father for it.

"Then do it quickly," he stated before leaving the room.

Monica stood, moved to Sam, extended her hand and waited. When he grasped it, she said, "I want daily reports on your findings."

Dominance, or should he say bossiness, definitely ran in the Lakefield family. "I'll keep Karena updated," he replied.

She lifted an elegantly arched brow then looked over her shoulder as she slipped her hand from his grasp. "Karena, I need to speak to you privately. I'll meet you in your office."

Turning back to Sam, she said, "Nice meeting you."

Monica walked away, and Sam felt the chill of air leaving behind her. This one was all business, no-nonsense and no softness. He remembered on the plane when Karena had told him about Monica being committed only to her job. She obviously hadn't lied, and he wondered briefly if his initial thought of introducing her to Alex Bennett was a smart move.

Alex was the oldest son of Marvin and Beatriz Bennett, the family he'd worked the stalking case for earlier this year. He was also the CEO of Bennett Industries and a bona fide workaholic. Still, Alex was Sam's brother-in-law since Bree had married his brother, Renny. Sam wasn't sure he'd wish the cold wrath of Monica Lakefield on a family member.

"For the record, I don't think tracing Leandro's call would have done you any good," he said when they were finally alone.

She was rubbing her temples, and she looked up at him as if she'd forgotten he was there. "I just don't know what else they expect me to do."

Her voice sounded so desolate, but then as if she'd released a deep, dark family secret, she straightened and walked toward him. "If you can just call me with your developments, that would be great. I just need to know for sure whom I met with and where that painting came from. As my father so eloquently stated, we'll pay you whatever is necessary for a speedy turnaround."

Was she dismissing him? Yes, she definitely was. Sam would have taken the hint if she hadn't looked so sad and so sexy at the same time. So instead of turning to leave the office, he reached out and took her free hand.

"I'll call you every day to let you know what I uncover." She looked up at him, confusion and something just a little darker in her eyes. Sam moved closer until his chest pushed the folder she was clutching against her breasts. "In fact, I'll call you twice a day, and you don't have to pay extra for that service."

Her nipples tingled and she stifled a groan. There was clothing between them and even that dammed folder, and still the heat from his body had mingled with hers, creating a fiery sphere around them. She inhaled deeply but the breath was ragged coming out, hitching on the huge swirl of sexual frustration mounting in the pit of her stomach.

God, she needed either a vibrator or a quickie right away. Before she did something clearly out of character and jumped Sam Desdune's bones.

Chapter 4

"So how long have you known him and are you sleeping with him?"

Monica was never one to beat around the bush, Karena thought the moment she stepped into her office and into Monica's barrage of questions.

"What are you talking about?" she asked, closing her office door behind her and praying none of the staff had been walking by and overheard.

"The P.I., Karena. How long have you known him?"

Monica sat in one of the guest chairs, her long legs crossed, arms resting on the sides.

Karena rounded her desk, dropped the folder then plopped down into her chair. "It's been a really long day, Monica. I'm not in the mood for your interrogations."

"Then you'd better get in the mood," Monica said, glaring at Karena. "Because if Daddy finds out you hired him because you're sleeping with him, he's going to go ballistic. And if this man doesn't figure out what the hell is going on with Leandro and that painting, we're both going to be out of a job."

"We're heirs to the company, Monica. How can we be out of a job?"

"That's a name on a piece of paper that rides on the fact that our father is still breathing."

Karena groaned, letting her head rest on the back of her chair. "It is not that serious, Monica, really."

"So you are sleeping with him," she accused.

Don't I wish. "No. I'm not sleeping with him. I met him a few months ago when I went to Maryland to visit a friend."

"What friend? Oh, that girl who's always getting herself into trouble."

"Noelle's not like that anymore. And this trouble she was in was serious, life-threatening serious. Sam and his partner helped her out."

"Sounds like you need to get better friends."

Karena was about to say something else when Monica held up a hand. "Don't get all uptight. I'm just trying to keep a handle on all this."

"D&D Investigations has a good reputation. I trust Sam to get to the bottom of this." And she did. From what she knew of him so far, he was a good investigator and a good friend. She only hoped her traitorous body could keep it together long enough for him to do the job.

"Well, you know how men are, so just be careful working with him," Monica quipped.

"What's that supposed to mean? I work with men all the time and I don't get this type of warning from you."

"The other men you work with all the time don't look at you like he was."

Karena flicked her wrist in Monica's direction as a way of dismissing her remark. "You're starting to sound melodramatic, like Deena."

"Oh, please, nobody is as melodramatic as Deena. I swear that girl lives in a world of her own."

"Well, she *is* a writer," Karena said in defense of their younger sister. Deena Lakefield was the free spirit of the family. Being cooped up behind a desk all day would have the same effect on her as kryptonite would on Superman, she thought with a smile.

"Deena doesn't know what she is from one day to the next." Monica stood. "Be that as it may, she's our lost cause of a sister no matter what. You, on the other hand, are salvageable and I don't want you getting your head all twisted over some man just because he looks good, smells good and watches you like you're the only woman on earth."

Her words had Karena sitting straight up in her chair. "He's all that, huh?"

Monica was not amused, although the corner of her mouth did lift in a smile. "He's not bad to look at, but you know my philosophy on men—especially good-looking men."

Yeah, Karena knew, and it was a damned shame. How a woman as strong as Monica could let one man tear her down and destroy her faith in the entire species was beyond her. "He's working for the company, Monica. That's all."

"Mmm-hmm," was her response as she walked out of the office.

"He's working for the company," Karena repeated once more when she was alone.

He's working for the company…*so why am I am thinking of his strong arms and how they'd feel wrapped tightly around me?*

He should have gone back to Connecticut immediately after leaving her office. Bree was there; he'd already called and briefed her on the situation. She would be working on it until it was time for her to leave for the day. Sam could go back to the office and help her or he could go home. Yet, it was almost six-thirty in the evening and he was still in Manhattan.

After leaving Lakefield Galleries he'd stopped at the library, using the Internet to retrieve a list of all art galleries in Manhattan and the surrounding boroughs. He wanted to know which ones were showing Leandro's work and which ones were trying to get more information on the man.

In the past few hours he'd visited six galleries, three of which had pieces of Leandro's on display, two that were negotiating to buy pieces and one that had tried valiantly to get in touch with Leandro's agent with no success.

Now Sam found himself turning into the same parking garage he'd been in earlier, heading back to Lakefield Galleries.

"Hi, we don't have a showing tonight so I'm just about to lock up," the friendly receptionist whose name he now knew was Astrid told him.

"I was hoping to catch Ms. Lakefield," he said. "Karena Lakefield," he amended when she stepped behind the desk and looked down at her computer screen.

"She hasn't logged off her computer yet so she's probably still here."

"Does she do that often?"

"Do what?"

"Work late," he said, realizing he'd spoken aloud. He'd been thinking that a woman as fine as Karena should have an active social life. Invitations to parties and friends to hang out with should be taking up the majority of her time.

Oh, no, that was his ex-fiancée's lifestyle he was thinking about. Leeza Purdy was the queen of Greenwich's most elite society clique, which meant that most of her time was spent entertaining. That was, when she could pry herself away from Sam's side, where she tried to dictate everything from the type of underwear he wore to the kind of gas he put into his car.

Breaking up with her had been one of his finer moments, and while his sisters had both readily told him that, he'd known it from the waves of relief that washed over him once it was all said and done.

Astrid shrugged. "Yes, I believe so. I'll walk you to her office," she said, picking up her purse and coming around the desk to meet him.

"Don't worry about it, I remember where it is. You go ahead and have a good evening."

"Thanks, you have a good evening, too. I'll put the automatic locks on so when you leave the door will lock behind you. As long as you're just going out, the security system will stay activated," Astrid said before slipping through the glass doors.

Sam nodded. He'd been wondering about their security, as he hadn't seen any cameras or security beacons on his first trip to the office. But now that he'd suspected someone was setting the Lakefields up to take a fall, he was determined to cover those bases.

When Astrid was gone, he moved behind her desk, kneeling to look underneath. There was a panic button. Good. Further inspection yielded a separate computer keyboard that Sam recognized as part of one of the better security systems. This keyboard monitored every employee in the office as they were logged in to their computers. It also monitored each office by using heat and motion sensors so that if someone were in an office that shouldn't be occupied, a message would immediately appear on a small computer screen.

Sam knew the system well and pressed a few keys before the screen flashed. The seventh floor was dedicated office space, he noted as he looked at the computerized layout. The larger rooms, he assumed, were conference rooms while the smaller ones were most likely employee offices. Of the ten offices, only two were still occupied. Karena and Monica, he knew without a doubt.

Tapping another sequence of keys, he pulled up the eighth floor, the gallery. This had additional security. Laser beams crisscrossed from the floor to the ceiling, in addition to the same heat and motion sensors that were on the office level. There were some smaller alcoves which had more security, coded keypads or locked encasements. He figured these probably held the more valuable pieces. He was just about to tap in another code when her voice startled him.

"What are you doing?"

His head snapped up, his body instantly warming at the sight of her.

"I was hungry," he said as casually as he could manage. "I figured you might be, too, so I came to take you to dinner."

She blinked, confusion marring her pretty face. "You're on the computer."

"No. I'm checking your security systems."

"Oh," she said and came around the desk to stand beside him. "The system was just updated two months ago."

He nodded. "It's a really good system, worth the money. How often do you and your sister stay here by yourselves?"

"We don't work normal hours, if that's what you're asking. But there's a security guard on the lower level of the garage and cameras everywhere. It's safe."

"It's not healthy," he replied, his fingers moving quickly over the keys as he closed the areas he'd wanted to check.

"It's after five and you're still working," she responded.

"Yeah, but I didn't leave my house until well after ten this morning. I'm betting you were here a lot earlier than that."

"That has nothing to do with your job," she said then moved around the desk.

He smiled at her sarcasm and her attempt to put him in his place. But she had no idea whom she was dealing with.

"You will find that I'm really into details. Whether they directly relate to my job doesn't really matter. Now, about dinner?"

"I'll order in. You can let yourself out," she was saying as he approached her.

"I don't want to eat alone."

"That's not my problem." Yet Karena got the sinking feeling that it was. His mouth said the hunger he spoke of was related to food. His eyes said something entirely different. The dark brown grew even darker, lust circling his irises with a smoldering ring. He approached her, and suddenly the reception area seemed too small for the both of them.

Inhaling sharply, she backed up, knowing instinctively that having him close to her was a mistake. He continued his trek forward, determination giving his tall, broad form an air of intimidation she wasn't quite sure she could handle.

"Are you afraid of me, Karena?"

Chapter 5

Karena let out a nervous chuckle. "Oh, please. Don't flatter yourself." Her back hit the wall and he kept right on moving until his body invaded what she needed to be her personal space. Her heart was pounding and she fought to keep her breathing normal. "I'm just trying to decide what's more important, getting to the bottom of this stolen-picture drama or kneeing you in the balls. What do you think?"

At the end of the day, training and upbringing aside, Sam was still a man. As such, he grimaced at the mere mention of the harm she threatened to his most prized possessions. "First, I'm not the enemy, so there's no need to run from me," he said calmly because he didn't know any other way. "Second, finding out what's going on with the painting is definitely important but not to the point that you neglect your own personal needs."

With one more step he was so close her perfume smelled as if it had been sprayed on him instead. She was a lot shorter than him, the top of her head coming to his pectoral muscles. Yet with his continued progress toward her, she'd lifted her chin and tilted her head so that she was staring directly into his eyes.

Sam realized in that moment that he wanted her beneath him, there was no question about it. He'd thought she was sexy the first two times he'd seen her, in a passing kind of way that all men noticed a good-looking woman. When he'd heard her voice on the phone this morning he'd thought, hell, maybe his chance at getting close to her was happening. Spending the day in Manhattan waiting like a schoolboy with a crush until it was time for her to get off from work to see her again proved he was going to lose the battle of taking things slow, which was normally his repertoire.

"Besides," he said, remembering her comment concerning his groin area because all the blood in his head was now rushing to that location, "kneeing me would be a dangerous option. Not to mention painful, and I'm sure it's not your intent to cause me pain."

She lifted a brow and he wanted to touch her there, to feel the smooth hairs just above her eyes. Anything to get his hands on her because his fingers itched to touch, his mouth watered to taste. "I'm hungry," he said, his voice hoarse.

Yes, he was, she thought, and so, quite possibly, was she. His body was pressed hard against hers now, his hands at her sides remaining still only by the control she saw straining at the surface. His body trembled with that control, that need to stay still battling with the desire to reach out and touch.

And, God, she wanted him to touch her. Never had she been weak to the needs of the flesh. With her mind made up about what type of men she would involve herself with and the limitations where relationships were concerned, Karena owned enough sex toys to open her own online sex shop. She used them more than she probably should and often wondered what effect all the electricity moving in and out of her body would have in the long run. Still, she was a woman and a professional who knew how to do what was necessary to survive in the world she'd built for herself.

Unfortunately, right about now she was so starved for the real thing, if Sam touched her she was bound to spontaneously combust, and then what?

Hadn't she just had this conversation with Monica? He was here for business and business only. She definitely needed to keep that thought in mind.

"Maybe you should leave," she said finally when the silence was giving her too much think time. "Go home, get yourself some dinner. Call me in the morning." And she would go home and try to figure out this mess she'd made of her career.

"I want you to join me," he persisted.

"We don't always get what we want, Sam." His name whispered past her lips and she watched as his eyes lowered to her mouth. Instinctively she licked her lips, then regretted the motion as Sam's head began to lower.

Oh, God, he was going to kiss her. He couldn't.

He was a breath away, warmth caressing her skin.

He shouldn't.

She braced herself, feeling the sizzling ache deep inside.

He wouldn't.

Oh, please, let his lips hurry up and touch hers.

When they did, all pleas were futile, all thought vanished and her mind clouded.

The taking was slow, his lips touching lightly against hers as if testing the waters. They touched hers a second time, and she was the one to step closer. Third time was the charm, as his tongue snaked out to meet with hers as if in silent agreement.

Warm, wet, enticingly slow, he kissed her and she kissed him right back.

Her hands clasped around his neck, his around her waist. The kiss deepened until his moans echoed in her ears, her heart thumped in her chest.

As far as kisses went this was, as Deena would say, off the chain.

His technique was slow, persistent and right on the mark as Karena felt sensations rippling fiercely throughout her body. This was breaking another of her rules when it came to men. She didn't do a lot of kissing. It was too intimate and stirred too many emotions. Like right now, she felt as if she was falling weightlessly into a swirling pit of desire lined with fluffy white clouds designed to make the fall smoother.

Heat licked at her with each stroke of his tongue as she felt his hold on her increasing until he was almost lifting her off the floor. His mouth opened over hers, devouring her lips, strangling her tongue. And still, she felt as if he was holding back, giving her only a taste…of what was to come.

Sam was lost, felt the stranglehold of control that normally surrounded him slipping just a bit. He hadn't meant to take the kiss this far, only to get a small taste. But she'd opened to him immediately, like a flower waiting to bloom. When she wrapped her arms around him, going higher on her tiptoes to meet his insistent embrace, he almost shivered.

He wasn't a player by any stretch of the imagination. He'd had only two serious relationships in his entire thirty-one years. Unlike his brother, Cole, his goals where women were concerned were already etched in stone. Love. Marriage. Family. That's what his parents had and that's what he wanted. Any woman he took to his bed more than once would have to know that right up front.

Damn, she tasted good and felt good, wrapped in his arms with her body pressed hotly against his own. Desire speared through him with an intensity that had him holding her tighter, tonguing her deeper. His erection throbbed and he lifted her until it was cradled against the flat indentation of her belly.

He could take her right here, right now, and give them both a pleasure they longed for. But that would be crass, not to mention unprofessional. No, he wanted the seductive Ms. Lakefield in his bed for hours on end, not propped up against this wall screaming his name, because that would never be enough.

With those thoughts running rapidly through his mind, Sam pulled away slightly, giving her a second to breathe before nipping her bottom lip, sucking it into his mouth and feeling her tremble once more. One more taste and he swore he was going to let her go. His tongue traced her lip, slid along the line of her teeth. She pulled her head back away from him and he groaned.

"Don't run, Karena," he whispered huskily, moving his lips closer to hers, his tongue already extended and waiting for her to join in.

For a split second it appeared she would back down, but then something sparked in her eyes and her tongue once again touched his, twirling around him in a sensual dance that had him moaning. His eyes were just closing once more, his mind slipping into the trance that her taste weaved around him, when his cell phone rang.

He'd planned to ignore it, Karena could tell by the way his arms tightened around her. She couldn't blame him, this was one helluva kiss. She'd felt it all the way down to the tingle in her toes. Yeah, that probably sounded real corny, but damn if she was lying. Sam Desdune definitely had skills in the kissing department, and if she wasn't careful she'd be ending her self-induced sexual drought right here in the lobby of her art gallery.

The phone chirped again and she forced herself to pull

back. "Answer it," she said, breathing hard and lifting a hand to wipe the moisture from her lips.

He only stared at her for a moment and she nodded toward the phone that still rang at his waist. Finally he reached for it but still kept her pinned to the wall.

"Desdune."

"I've got identification and a passport. Are you near a fax?" Bree said in her efficient way.

"What's the fax number?" he asked Karena and repeated it to Bree.

"That's the machine in my office," Karena said, using this diversion as an opportunity to slip away from him and move in the direction of her office.

Grateful for the space she walked quickly, knowing he was watching her but refusing to bask in the feeling of sexiness that emanated with just one look from him. She wasn't an amateur in the game of boy meets girl, boy likes girl, boy and girl have sex. And after what they'd just done she was thinking more and more that sleeping with Sam Desdune would be just as explosive as the kiss they'd shared. Her business-only stance might have to be readjusted.

Pushing through the door to her office, she saw that whatever he'd asked be faxed to them was already being transmitted through the machine.

"Your office works fast," Karena quipped.

"It's Bree, my twin sister. She takes her job about as seriously as you take yours."

"Smart woman," she said, lifting the first page from the machine without looking at him.

He was about to say something else when she gasped.

"It's not him."

He moved closer to her. "What?"

She handed him the paper, dread filling her eyes, her entire body tense. "That's not the man I met with in Brazil. It wasn't Leandro. Monica was right. I got played."

Chapter 6

"You're blaming yourself for something that could have happened to anyone," Sam said as they sat in one of his favorite restaurants in the city, 212.

He'd ordered steamed shrimp dumplings while Karena had Asian-style tuna rolls that she was barely touching.

"I should have known better," she said, her elbows propped on the table, chin resting on her clasped hands as she stared just past him contemplatively.

"How? Nobody's ever seen this guy. There's no way you could have expected this type of duplicity. And you don't strike me as the kind of woman to bask in self-pity, so what's really going on?"

She blinked, his words catching her off guard. Sam Desdune was more than unexpected. Not only was she extremely attracted to him, a fact evidenced by the wanton manner in which she'd kissed him only an hour or so earlier, but his whole demeanor was different from what she would have anticipated.

Of course, she'd known he was easy to talk to; the two times she'd seen him before were proof of that. They'd slipped into conversation as if they'd known each other for years. Yet, today there was something else.

"It's my dad," she found herself saying as a result of this strange comfort zone between them. "He's…um…" Her voice trailed off.

"Difficult," Sam finished for her.

She couldn't help but smile. His insight was uncanny. "For lack of a better word, yes."

"Is that just with you or does he treat everyone he knows in that condescending way?"

"Oh, no." She was already shaking her head. She didn't want Sam to get the wrong idea about her family. "He's really not that bad all the time." Why she felt the need to defend him she didn't know. "The business is just his life, so he's very protective of it."

"He owns the galleries and the Lakefield Foundation?"

How did he know about the foundation? *Duh, he's a private investigator.* But why investigate the Lakefields? *Better to deal with the matter at hand, Karena, stop borrowing trouble.* That's a problem she'd had all her life, according to her mother.

"The foundation was instituted about five years ago with the goal of entering into philanthropic arenas. My father comes from a colorful background, his ancestors building off the luck of the land, so to speak. So he and his brothers decided it was time to give something back."

"And his brothers are a part of the foundation, as well?"

He was steadily eating and it wasn't rude; they were at dinner, after all. He forked his food, watched her as he chewed, asked her questions and every now and then glanced at her plate as if telling her she should be doing the same thing.

With a shrug she picked up a tuna roll, inhaled the fragrant aroma and took a bite. It tasted as good as it smelled and she almost smiled as her stomach churned in appreciation. She hadn't eaten all day, she was so worried over this painting issue.

"Yes, my dad has two brothers. They both live here in New York and all of them got their start in the steel business. Now their corporations are basically run by my cousins, so the uncles are just as bored as my father."

Sam nodded. "When my father gets bored he cooks. Then he changes the menu at the restaurants. His managers and chefs hate when he does that, especially my brother, Cole."

"You're from a large family, right?" she asked, finishing off one roll then using her fork to sample the spinach salad that came with her entrée.

"I'm one of four children. My parents are from New Orleans, where the Desdune lineage could probably occupy two or three counties." He chuckled at that, sipped his wine and used his napkin to wipe his fingers.

His plate was clear, she noticed with amazement. Well, he'd said he was hungry.

"Ever heard of Lucien's, the Creole-and-Cajun restaurant? There's one in Harlem," he told her.

"There sure is," she said when she'd finished chewing. The dressing was excellent, and Karena found herself enjoying the meal as well as the company. "I've been there a few times. The ham with bourbon-pecan sauce is fantastic."

He smiled proudly. "One of my father's favorite dishes. My brother—he's the next to the oldest—manages the Greenwich restaurant. There's one in New Orleans and another one in Atlanta."

"You said you had a twin. Are you and she the oldest?"

"No. Bree and I are the youngest children. Lynn's my oldest sister."

"And you and Bree are the only two who didn't go into the restaurant business?"

"Lynn's a family-law attorney. Cole's the only one who followed my dad's footsteps."

"Really?" That was interesting. "So what does your mother do?"

"What doesn't she do?" He chuckled. "She has her hand in everything, from the restaurants to the hundreds of committees in Greenwich where we live, to the charities she likes to work with. I swear I don't know how she does it. She's like the Energizer Bunny pumped with adrenaline."

Karena laughed, the tiny sound bubbling from her chest, reaching her eyes and stretching across the table, taking Sam's breath away.

"What about your mother, what does she do while you and your sisters are working with your father?" he asked suddenly, wanting to know everything he could about her.

Sitting back in her chair, she finished chewing and lifted her glass to take a drink. Her smile had dissipated slightly as she seemed to contemplate her response. "Well, for starters we've had a sibling defect from the family business, as well. Deena, my youngest sister, isn't all that interested in the gallery, or the foundation for that matter. My mother believes that Deena is still trying to find herself. Monica thinks she's flighty, and my father, well, unfortunately Deena wasn't a son, so he pays her about as much attention as he does me and Monica. No, less, since Deena makes a habit of not showing up for family functions."

"I see." And he really did. The Lakefields were like most families, united yet divided, loving yet judgmental. He wondered how that affected Karena. "What do you think about Deena's not going into the family business?"

She sighed. "I think she has a right to follow her dreams. If that doesn't encompass working in an art gallery or finding a cause to fight for, then that's her prerogative. I also think there's a measure of family loyalty to consider."

Interesting, Sam thought. "Really? How far do you think you should take family loyalty? Should you sacrifice your own wants and needs for the approval of your family?"

"That's not what I said," she snapped.

Sam watched her carefully. There was a lot she wasn't saying. Curiosity had killed the cat—when he'd first gone into P.I. work, he'd had a plaque on his wall that said that very thing. However, curiosity had also begun to pay his bills.

"I work at the galleries because I love art. I enjoy selecting the right pieces and showcasing them. I'm not much for the charities and planning fundraisers, so I steer clear of that. That's why I can respect Deena's choice to do whatever she decides to do. But sometimes I think she's a little too hard on us. We do and say things most times because we care about her."

"That's usually the way it is with family." He nodded, and then because she'd still managed to talk about everyone else in her family but her mother, he said, "Your mother is interested in art?"

She shook her head. "No."

"The foundation?"

"No."

Short and to the point. This was definitely something she didn't want to talk about. He could push, it was in his nature to do just that, but at that very moment her gaze shifted down to her lap. The tip of her tongue was barely visible as she licked her lips, and Sam's entire body tightened. Suddenly, talking about her family wasn't of the utmost importance.

"Ready to go home?" he asked and was rewarded by a shocked but clearly aroused gaze from her.

* * *

Karena's apartment was on West End Place in the city. She'd chosen this place for its proximity to the gallery and Riverside and Central Parks. Early on Sunday mornings she'd go running in either park, because that seemed to be the only free time she could find for herself. And even then more than an hour or two was unheard of.

With her stomach full and her senses on overload from Sam's close proximity, she used the key to enter her apartment. Dropping her purse and briefcase on the table near the door, she picked up a remote control and pressed the button that would illuminate the living- and dining-room areas.

"Soooo," she began, rubbing her now-damp palms over her thighs. "Thanks for dinner and thanks for seeing me home." *And thanks for getting me so aroused I'm now a certified bundle of nerves.*

"Great place," he said, ignoring her hint and moving around her to peruse the living room.

Stifling a sigh, Karena turned and walked behind him. She would not look at him, not at the way the muscles in his back pressed against the material of his shirt in such an enticing manner or the way his butt looked in his slacks. She needed a game plan, she thought hastily.

"I wanted to be close to the park," she said.

He turned to face her, the wall full of windows showcasing the breathtaking New York skyline at night surrounding him. "And to your job."

Narrowing her gaze, she did sigh this time. "Ok, you've already expressed your dislike of how dedicated I am to my job. Can we talk about something else now?"

To her surprise, he shrugged then moved into the dining room. "Not one for color are you?"

"What?" She was shaking her head. There were times today when Sam Desdune had been so easy to read—the times when he was leering at her with that sexual hunger that even now had her nipples tingling. And then there were times like right this moment when he seemed to go casually from one annoying subject to the next—as if he anticipated her answers and didn't give them much credence.

"Your decor," he said with a flourish of one arm indicating her furniture. "Everything's one color. Cream. Subtle, safe, neutral."

Folding her arms across her chest, she replied, "I like it."

He walked toward her then extended both his hands to touch her wrists. Unfolding her arms, he wrapped his fingers slowly around her wrists. "I like you," he whispered.

"You're confusing me," she said. Her mind was so full of contradictions where he was concerned. Calling him was business, meeting with him this afternoon was, as well. Kissing him was insane, and way too enjoyable. Dinner was being cordial. Standing with him, here in the center of her apartment not three inches away from him, while moonlight mixed with the soft artificial glow of the lamp danced through the room, was…dangerous.

"Am I?" His voice was a low rumble, the intent in his eyes clear as water.

"I don't like to be confused. I don't like not knowing what's going on."

He nodded. "That's a fair-enough admission. So how about I tell you what's going on."

She smiled nervously. "Why don't you do that."

His thumbs were whispering over the backs of her hands as he spoke, his dark brown gaze holding hers. "I'm really attracted to you. I have been since first meeting you at Noelle and Brock's place."

"Sam," she started.

"Shhh. Don't interrupt." Releasing one of her hands, he used a finger to touch her lips. "Seeing you again at the Gramercy's opening only incited the urge to touch you once more."

She looked away, and Sam used a finger to her chin to guide her face back to him. "And when you called today I thought this had to be fate. You see, my Creole grandmother, Ruby, is really big on signs and destinies and all that. Me, I just follow my gut."

His fingers brushed softly over her jawline and Karena felt her whole body begin to shiver. "I called you because I needed your help…with the painting. It's…ah…this…is just business."

He smiled, slow and knowingly. Again her response seemed anticipated. His was not.

"This is much more than business," he whispered seconds before his lips were once again on hers.

Chapter 7

His lips were like slow heat, parting hers until he extended his tongue. He tasted like wine, tangy and just a touch sweet. Her eyelids fluttered closed and she knew she was sinking fast.

His arms were around her, not resting seductively at the base of her back but slipping farther down, grasping her bottom until she was lifted from the floor and pressed against his rigid erection.

She tried to speak but her open mouth was only an invitation to him. Tilting her head to the side, she accepted his tongue, twisting and twirling her own around his as her arms went around his neck.

This was personal, too damned personal. He wasn't only kissing her—he was touching her, intimately. Touching a part of her that she'd carefully kept under lock and key.

It was lust. Plain and simple. She needed to get some… soon. That's what Noelle would say. Hell, that's what she'd told Noelle only a few months ago when she was debating what to do about Brock Remington. Now the two of them were happily tucked into their lakefront home blissfully in love.

But love wasn't for Karena. Not if the price she would pay for it started with losing her identity, as her mother had. Surely she was getting ahead of herself, borrowing trouble again. This was just about sex. Sam wasn't looking for forever. Or was he? It didn't matter. That's definitely not what she was looking for.

So as hard as it was, she unwrapped her arms from around his neck, used her elbows to push against his chest and twisted her lips away from his.

Unfortunately, Sam wasn't catching her drift.

"I told you not to run from me," he said, his teeth nipping the heated skin of her neck.

"I'm not running. I'm stopping this insanity," she said and squirmed a little more until he set her down on her feet again. He kept his arms tightly around her but her lips were no longer held captive by his, thank goodness. "Let me go."

"So you can gather your armor and shut yourself off from the inevitable? I don't think so."

"Fine. Then stand here with your hands on me while I scream to the top of my lungs and we'll both wait until the security guard at the end of the hall comes rushing in with his gun raised."

She thought she had him there, but he simply lifted a brow then chuckled.

"First of all, rent-a-cop down the hall doesn't have a gun. He has pepper spray, which is pretty damn bad with the right aim. But I, however, have this."

He reached behind his back and pulled out a black gun that looked way too dangerous for him to have casually tucked in the back of his pants.

Shrugging, he put the gun back and kept smiling at her. "Now, you don't have to scream, because I'm not in the habit of forcing women to do my bidding."

"Good," she snapped and used the moment when only one of his hands was on her to break free of his hold. It was too easy, she wasn't fool enough to believe otherwise. He'd let her go, although his gaze all but held her still.

"Like I said, this is business and we can discuss it further tomorrow."

"No. Business was earlier. This—" the hand that had restored his gun to his back now slid sinuously around to his abs, then lower to just over his belt buckle "—this is definitely personal and definitely not going to wait until tomorrow."

She swallowed deeply and felt a clutching in her center. This was way too much for her to handle. Her own relationship hang-ups aside, Monica's warning resounded in her head, punctuating another reason why she couldn't lose control with Sam Desdune. "I ah…I need…um…a minute."

It was cowardice, Karena knew and hated that fact. Still, hurrying past him, she didn't wait for a response. That probably worked out for the best, because she wouldn't have liked the smile that spread across his face.

She was definitely running, Sam thought the moment he was left alone in her living room. And he was no woman chaser. Never had been and never would be.

Okay, that statement would have been much stronger if he wasn't at this very moment walking in the same direction Karena had just fled to.

She'd gone through a door and this was the only one closed, he thought, after walking down the short hallway. Raising his fist, he figured he should knock but decided against it. She'd only run again.

Sam knew he was attracted to her and he knew she was

attracted to him. He hadn't lied when he said he didn't force women. He didn't. But he wouldn't let one lie to him, either. Especially not when her only reason for denying their attraction was rooted in some strictly business mumbo jumbo.

So he turned the knob and pushed the door open. What he saw had him rethinking the whole make-her-see-reason plan.

Standing at the foot of a king-size bed cloaked in a—yes, he should have expected—cream satin comforter, was Karena. That wasn't what shocked him. It was what she held in her hand that had his penis throbbing, pressing painfully against his zipper.

"What are you doing?" She turned to face him, her hands going instantly behind her back.

Sam took three long strides to her, reached behind her back and, with a little resistance from her, managed to pull both her hands and what she held in them around so he could get a closer look.

There had to be some medical issue with an erection as hard and heated as his was now.

"What are you going to do with this?"

She opened her mouth to speak then closed it again. Her tongue snaked out slowly, swiping her lower lip as her fingers still gripped the vibrator in her right hand.

"You would rather come in here and use this than stay with me and accept the real thing?"

She shook her head quickly. "No. I wasn't using it. I was putting it away. I came in here to give us some space because I'd rather not start something that neither of us can afford to finish."

"I don't know about you, but I fully intend to finish—"

"No!" Pulling away, she cut him off. "This is not how this is going to go down."

He let her move away because she looked tense. Actually,

she looked sexy as hell holding a vibrator and standing in her bedroom with her shoes off and her face flushed with arousal. Still, he sensed the struggle in her and thought it best to allow her this bit of space, this final moment of denial.

"I can't get involved with you," she started quickly then turned away from him. "I can't get involved with anyone. Not right now, I mean. There's still so much I need to do for myself, in my career. And it's just not the right time for romantic entanglements."

That little speech almost sounded rehearsed. "I don't recall asking for romantic entanglements. I think we're on a more basic level here."

She was nodding her head. "Yeah, sex. I know. Look," she said, turning back to him. "I feel it, too. Okay, I'll admit that we're attracted to each other. *Very* attracted to each other. But getting together, even on a basic level, isn't good for us. We have to get to the bottom of this painting issue and—"

"And you're blowing this way out of proportion," he said, taking a chance to move closer to her. "So let's slow down and take it one step at a time."

She took a deep breath when he stood in front of her and let it out shakily.

"Right. Maybe I am overreacting. I don't know what's wrong with me."

"I do," he said slowly. "And I know just how to fix it."

Touching a palm to her face, he saw the moment she began to put her shields up again. "No. Don't. Just relax."

"Sam."

"Shhh. I said relax. I know what you need."

And with those words he let his hand fall from her cheek to her shoulder. "Go sit on the bed."

She looked quizzically at him.

"Trust me, Karena. I won't do anything that you don't approve of. Now, go sit on the bed."

She was contemplating. He could see it in her eyes. When she finally decided to move to the bed, he almost laughed. Damn, but she was stubborn.

When she plopped down onto the bed like an angry teenager, tossing the vibrator onto the pillow, he thought about abandoning the whole wicked idea he'd come up with. She didn't want a romantic entanglement, she'd just told him that. And what did he want? Right now he wanted more than air itself to strip, get onto that bed with her and bury himself so deep inside her neither of them remembered their names—let alone the reasons why they shouldn't be together.

But he was smart enough to know something a lot of men chose to forget—when it was time to put his own needs aside for the sake of a pretty lady.

"I'm going to touch you, Karena." That was probably an understatement.

"And?" she asked cautiously.

"I'm going to undress you."

Her hands were in her lap but fell to her sides to rest on the mattress at his words.

"And then I'm going to touch you some more."

She lifted a brow as he moved closer to her.

"You think what I need is for you to touch me? Funny, you didn't strike me as an arrogant man."

Her joking tone was probably meant to mask the reservations she still had, but it only served to arouse him more.

"Not arrogant, just confident."

She shrugged. "Same difference."

"Stop talking." He was kneeling in front of her now, pushing her dress up her thighs. Again she arched an eyebrow but didn't speak.

Dragging his hands and the material up and over her waist, he pulled the dress over her head. Sucking in a breath, he tried not to be the one behaving like a teenager at the sight of her.

Great breasts, slim waist and, although he couldn't see it, he knew her bottom was just as perfect as the rest of her.

After tossing the dress to the floor, he reached for the band of her stockings, pulling it along with her panties down her legs, stopping briefly to kiss the arch of each of her feet as he slipped the silken material free.

Other than a gasp, Karena remained quiet and cooperative. Because he couldn't resist, he leaned forward and kissed her. "You're gorgeous. Did you know that?"

She laughed nervously. "No. But thanks for telling me."

"Anytime," he said, tracing a heated line with his tongue over her chin and down to her neck before pushing her back on the bed.

"Now I want you to lie still and let me give you what you need."

"Sam—"

"Karena, I'm not going to hurt you. Trust me. Can you do that?"

"I don't know you and you don't know me."

He tilted his head to the side. "I know that you're one of three daughters born to a really stubborn but successful man. I know that you work so hard you forget to eat. I know that there is nothing more important to you than your family. And I know you like when I do this." His lips touched hers lightly, then his tongue traced an outline around them. Just as he expected, she shivered beneath him.

"I know you, Karena. And you know me," his voice was a hoarse whisper. "Don't you?"

A small cry escaped her throat and she began to speak, slowly. "I know that you're one of four children," she whispered, her eyes clouding with desire as she looked up at him. "That your twin sister works with you and drives you crazy. I know that you have a healthy appetite for food and that you like to be in control."

With a hand in the center of her chest, he unhooked her bra while smiling down at her. "Then I'd say we know each other pretty damn well. So don't worry. Whenever you want me to stop, just say the word."

"And you'll stop?" she asked timidly.

He groaned. "I'm probably going to hate it like a bee sting, but if you tell me to stop, trust that I will."

For endless seconds his gaze probed hers. Until she nodded her agreement.

Palming each of her breasts in his hands, he watched her chocolate-brown nipples pucker. With much restraint he leaned forward, kissing each one. The moment she started to squirm, he pulled away and reached for the vibrator.

Switching it on, he used one hand to lift her leg, planting her foot on the mattress. After positioning the other leg the same way, he licked his own lips at the sight before him. Gorgeous didn't quite say it completely. What was it about this woman that modern-day adjectives couldn't describe?

When his gaze moved down farther to stop at the juncture between her legs, Sam's breath caught and lodged somewhere between his lungs and his brain. He had to close his eyes once, then reopen them before daring to speak. And even when words formed in his mind, he didn't quite know what to say.

"Good Lord, you're trying to kill me," he finally breathed.

She was bare—well, slick with desire, but otherwise shaved bare—and his already burgeoning erection throbbed.

Without preamble Sam lowered his head, placing what could only be described as the world's sweetest kiss on Karena's most private part. Every reason she'd come up with to walk away from him and this attraction simply melted away. In the distance she could hear the persistent hum of her vibrator, but all she could focus on was the warmth of his mouth on her.

Then he replaced his lips with the vibrator, moving it along her slick folds, and she moaned. She'd done this more times than she could count when she was alone. Yet tonight it felt different.

"So sweet," he whispered and let the vibrator's tip touch her center entrance while his tongue slid slowly over the tightened bud of her juncture once more.

"My God, Sam. Now who's trying to kill who?"

"Easy, sweetness," he crooned, one hand pressing against the thigh she'd tightened against his head. "Easy. I know what you need."

"Then give it to me!" she screamed and wondered who the primal-sounding voice belonged to.

Be careful what you wish for, was another one of her mother's favorite sayings.

Those words echoed in Karena's mind as Sam slipped the vibrator inside her quaking center while simultaneously suckling her tender folds.

Her release was quick, electrifying and damn-near lethal as Karena arched her back and screamed Sam's name.

Chapter 8

He'd left her.

As unbelievable as it seemed, after helping Karena into the shower and waiting until she'd finished so he could tuck her into bed, Sam had let himself out of her apartment.

All the way to his car he could imagine Cole's crass jokes if he'd dared tell his brother about tonight's escapade. Luckily for him, kissing and telling was a long-gone pastime for him.

The ride back to Connecticut took less than an hour. It was late, so traffic had died down significantly. Thoughts of Karena and the events of the day circled in his mind. When he'd awakened this morning it had been to plans of playing with Romeo, maybe stopping by his parents' house and checking in at the office late in the afternoon.

Then the phone call had come, and like a moth to a flame he'd been drawn to her. She needed him and he'd gone running. But Sam had no idea how deep Karena Lakefield's needs actually went.

Sure there was the problem with the stolen artwork, but Sam was confident he, along with Bree and Bailey, could get to the bottom of that. On another, more personal level, however, Sam was considering his next move.

She was an intelligent woman, one who knew what she wanted and how to get it, hence her own personal vibrator. Karena didn't need a living, breathing man, not in her career and not in her personal life. At least that's what she wanted to believe. Sam wasn't quite sure why.

Maybe an ex-boyfriend had broken her heart. Maybe she was just picky. From the way he'd watched her at work, she'd probably say she was too busy for men or relationships.

None of those reasons rang true for him.

Turning into his driveway, Sam switched off the ignition and sat for a moment, his decision made. Whatever was behind her half-hearted attempts to pull away from him, he was going to make her see reason. He was going to seduce Karena Lakefield. Hell, he'd already taken the first step to that tonight, so the decision was actually obvious.

The minute he opened the door Romeo was there, lumbering his big-but-lithe body over to Sam, lifting his head and sniffing.

"No snacks for you, champ. Sorry. I know it's late." He rubbed Romeo between his ears and turned to move toward the kitchen. "Come on, let's get you something to eat."

Romeo, although hungry, didn't move. Instead he barked to get Sam's full attention. Stopping, Sam looked down at his dog, then to the envelope on the floor near Romeo's left paw.

"You got the mail while I was out," he joked then bent down to pick up the envelope, wondering why it wasn't in the locked mailbox at the end of his driveway. Somebody had come all the way to his front door and slipped the envelope beneath it. Whatever was in this letter must have been important.

Sam opened it as he walked, pausing at the threshold of the kitchen when he saw the scrawling script. It was an invitation to the Greenwich Country Club's Fall Brunch. He was about to ball it up and toss it when the handwritten note on the back caught his eye.

"I've already RSVP'd for us. Give me a call to let me know what time you're picking me up."

Leeza. He sighed then proceeded to ball the invitation in one hand, rubbing the back of his neck with the other.

He'd broken up with Leeza months ago. Sat her down and told her that their relationship—engagement—was over. Why? Because she was driving him insane with her controlling nature.

Leeza Purdy was from a prominent family in Greenwich. She went to the best schools, wore the best clothes, drove the best car. In her mind, the struggle to be the best at all times was first and foremost. Why she wanted Sam, who was born of a great family with money of their own, but with his municipal police detective job, he hadn't understood in the beginning.

But after dating her for a year Sam had thought their social status, rules and etiquettes were secondary to the love they shared for each other. Fortunately, Sam learned before it was too late that they were not meant to be. It was too bad that Leeza hadn't received that memo.

"Well, I'm glad one of us is living happily ever after," Karena said and instantly wished she'd kept her mouth shut.

She was on the phone with her best friend, Noelle Vincent, who now lived in Maryland with her boyfriend, Brock Remington. It was because of Noelle that she'd met Sam. So she could probably blame the conflicting mood she was in this morning on her. Somehow Karena knew that wasn't going to work.

"Hmm, sounds like trouble brewing," Noelle said. "What's

going on? Is your dad on the warpath again? Or is it Monica? Girl, when are you going to find her a man to calm her down?" Noelle chuckled.

Karena couldn't hold back her own smile. Monica did need a man. Now, Karena knew that her older sister had been through something bad with her boyfriend, three years ago, but it was past time she let that go and moved on. Monica had never told her or any of the family what really happened with her ex, but whatever it was it had turned Monica off men totally. Karena often wondered if she should just give Monica the Web site from which she purchased all her little sex toys.

That thought alone had Karena groaning. The memory of what Sam had done with that vibrator still haunted her, causing her knees to close so tightly she heard the bones knock beneath the desk.

"There's nothing I can do for Monica. I fear she's a lost cause."

"Nobody's a lost cause."

"Spoken like a woman in love," Karena said with a smile. She was genuinely happy for Noelle. She liked Brock and thought the change of scenery and a mature relationship was good for her friend. Unfortunately, her life wasn't so easily handled.

"No, spoken like an optimistic person. Why are you always looking for the bad, expecting the worse?"

Karena rubbed her temple. "Because it's always there."

"So is happiness, you could try searching for that."

"Or I could stay on the path I'm already on."

"And what's that, the independent career woman who sleeps alone?"

"Sleeping with a man is not all it's cracked up to be."

"Of course not if you're just sleeping."

They both laughed at that.

"Please, I have enough toys to start my own store. I'm not starving in the sex department."

"No. Just the companionship department." Noelle sighed heavily. "So is that what your mood is about? You need a man?"

"Noelle, I do not need a man. Why do all women think that? I'm complete without somebody with a penis and an arrogant attitude waking up beside me every morning. I have a job, I pay all my own bills. My apartment is nice, my car is paid for. I do not need a man to complete or define me."

"Ooookay, let me know when you're ready to exhale."

Karena slammed back in her chair. It started to spin a little so that now her back was facing her closed office door. "Sorry. That wasn't necessary. I'm just so tired of the assumption that every woman needs a man."

"Then let's use another word. Let's say you want a man?"

"Yeah right, like I want the hives or a root canal."

Noelle laughed loud and long. "Comparing a man to hives or a root canal, that can only mean one thing."

"What?"

"That you met someone."

"I did not meet someone." Karena was quiet for a moment. "I already knew him."

"I knew it! I knew it. Tell me all about him."

She was going to regret this, she knew, but she needed somebody to talk to, and her sisters were definitely out of the question. The funny thing was just a few months ago the tables were turned. She was the one giving Noelle advice on her love life. The difference now was that Karena didn't have a love life. What she had was a stolen painting and a man who could kiss her into an orgasm but preferred to apply double pressure with his mouth and her prized sex toy. What had she gotten herself into?

"Okay, I'm going to tell you, but again I don't want you going overboard. This is not a love connection, Noelle. It's just a situation. One that I need your honest advice on. So take off those love blinders you have on and give me your unbiased opinion."

"Ooooh, this is serious."

Karena laughed. This is why she and Noelle were good friends. Noelle was feisty and upbeat, smart and witty, bold and tenacious. All Karena could claim to be was intelligent and ambitious. The rest she sort of let her sisters handle.

"I went to Brazil and bought a painting. Now it seems the painting might be stolen. So I called Sam Desdune to investigate for me."

"Uh-huh?"

"He came to the office yesterday. He left. Then he came back, took me to dinner and took me home."

"And?"

Karena inhaled then let the breath out slowly. "He caught me with my vibrator in hand and used it to make me come harder and longer than I ever have before," she said, quickly closing her eyes as if that were going to temper Noelle's response.

"What!" Noelle screeched.

"Wait a minute, back up, rewind, he did what to you? Sam Desdune? The quiet private investigator who works with Trent? The one with the wholesome good looks and killer smile?"

"You know who he is, Noelle."

"Yeah, I know who he is. I'm trying to get a handle on what you've just told me he did. So why did you have the vibrator? Was it in your purse? And what type was it, because I have one but I was thinking of getting an upgrade."

Karena rolled her eyes. "Noelle, can you please concentrate on the matter at hand?"

"I am. I mean, I thought we were talking about Sam and the great sex you had."

"No. I did not say we had sex. I said he used the vibrator on me and…his hands…his mouth."

"Oooo, girl, this is too good." Noelle was laughing again.

Karena was beginning to feel like a comedienne for all the enjoyment Noelle was getting from their conversation. "Look, Sam is supposed to find out what's going on with this painting. Not what's going on with me and my desires."

"At least you're admitting you have desires."

"I'm not dead, Noelle. Of course I have desires. That's why I have the toys."

"The ones that he used on you."

"Girl, you truly have a one-track mind."

"Okay, okay. So your problem is that you want to keep this business-only but your libido is getting in the way."

"Yes."

"Well, it's clearly too late for keeping this business. So now what you need to figure out is how to play things from here. You still want to sleep with him, don't you?"

"There's no need in lying, especially to you. Yes, I want to sleep with him."

"So do it."

"Just like that?"

"Yeah, just like that. You told me once that Brock and I were both consenting adults, so there was no real reason why we couldn't act on our attraction to each other. Now I'm telling you the same thing."

"But it's different for me."

"Why?"

"Because," Karena got quiet. "Because I'm afraid that I could really fall for a man like Sam."

"Really? What kind of man is he?"

"He loves his family for one and he's loyal to them, I can tell. He's fair and he's confident. He's honest."

"And he looks good in dress clothes and jeans," Noelle added.

"What? How do you know Ms. Two-Steps-Away-From-Being-Married?"

"I'm not blind and I've seen him a couple of times, so I know. Anyway, all that sounds like good stuff. What are the cons to hooking up with him?"

Because Karena had thought about this one issue all night after Sam left her apartment and then again this morning when she'd awakened, it was on the tip of her tongue when Noelle asked. And because Noelle was her closest friend and probably the only person she could talk to about this, she said, "Because I don't want to end up like her. I don't want to fall in love with a man and give him every part of me until there's nothing left. I just don't want to make that mistake."

"What mistake don't you want to make?"

Karena nearly jumped out of her chair, the phone receiver slipping from her hand as she turned to see none other than Noreen Lakefield standing in the doorway.

"Ah…hi, Mom."

Chapter 9

Noreen Henson Lakefield was a gentle woman, her silver-streaked hair styled in loose curls that rested just below her ears. Just about five feet four inches in heels, she wore a navy blue skirt suit with a paisley-print blouse beneath. Her complexion was like a cup of coffee with light cream. And just as when they were kids, her eyes were all-seeing, her ears all-hearing.

"Nothing," Karena said, answering her mother hastily. "Noelle, I'll give you a call back." After hearing Noelle's goodbye, she placed the receiver on the base as slowly as she could. Buying time.

How much had her mother overhead? The office door had been closed, or pushed very close to being closed. So she could have possibly heard the entire conversation, well, Karena's portion. Or she could have only heard the ending. Or...

"You're thinking too much, Karena," Noreen said, putting her Hermes purse on one of the guest chairs while taking a seat in the other. "You always get that crease across your forehead when you think too much. If you're not careful, it'll freeze there and you'll look deformed."

Karena couldn't help but chuckle. "Did you come all the way into the city to tell me to stop worrying and stop frowning?"

Noreen looked up sharply, then folded her hands on her lap. "No. I came to see how my child was doing. Is there a crime in that?"

"No, ma'am," Karena said quickly, unsure of Noreen's mood at the moment. Usually her mother was all smiles and soft-spoken. If there were two things Karena could count on when she was growing up, it was that on Sunday mornings Noreen would be shaking her to get up for Sunday school at eight in the morning and that her mother's voice would never be raised above polite-conversation level. Today, something seemed different.

"Good. Because I'd hate to think I was a prisoner in my own home."

Karena stared at her mother quizzically, then caught herself because she knew she was frowning again. "So, how are you?" she asked cautiously.

"I'm just fine," Noreen almost snapped.

Then she took a deep breath. Karena watched as her mother's ample bosom rose and fell, her hands—the left one wearing only the magnificent diamonds her father had given her—smoothing down her thighs.

"I'm not fine," Noreen said finally.

Karena immediately leaned forward, elbows resting on her desk blotter. "What's going on? Are you sick?" Her heart had already begun beating erratically at the mere thought of illness claiming her mother.

"No. No." Noreen shook her head and lifted a hand as if to wave that notion out of Karena's mind. "Nothing like that. I'm as healthy as a thirty-year-old. Just trapped in a fifty-seven-year-old body." She gave a wry chuckle.

"I guess trapped is as good a word as any," Noreen continued.

"Mama, you're scaring me," Karena admitted.

"I know, I'm scaring myself being so dramatic, just like—"

Karena was already smiling as she finished her mother's sentence. "Deena. I know. How is she, by the way? Last I heard she had meetings with a literary agent. That was a few weeks ago."

"Yes, that's what she's been up to, trying to find an agent to sell a book she's written."

"The romance story," Karena said, nodding and remembering her younger sister calling her late one evening with this idea for an older man falling for a younger, less-mature woman. Karena vaguely remembered telling her that happened every day and what would make the story so different that people would want to pay to read about it. Her comments had fallen on deaf ears, as about two months later Deena had informed her that she'd finished the book. Karena, being the dedicated and slightly interested big sister, read the manuscript and was surprisingly pleased. Deena may have finally found her niche.

"I think she's really going to do something good this time." Noreen's words interrupted Karena's thoughts.

"Yeah, I think so, too."

"I think it's time I did something good, also."

Her words were spoken quietly as Noreen looked down at her hands and back up at Karena. "When we started the Lakefield Foundation I had so many ideas of things I wanted to do. You girls are grown now, and that house seems so big now for just me and your father. You know Paul has to have his staff, so there's not much for me to do. But I wanted to do something. I wanted it so badly."

Karena couldn't hide her shock. Her mother had always been—just that, her mother. She'd cooked for them when they were young, picked out and ironed their clothes every day—against their father's wishes, albeit. She'd helped them with homework when they came home, watched them play outside and drove them to whatever extracurricular activities they were a part of. But never had she worked a nine-to-five job, never had she left them for business meetings or made business-related excuses about why she couldn't do something with or for them. She'd always been there for her children and her husband. A fact that sent a chill running down Karena's spine.

"I still want to do something."

"Then do it." The words rushed out of Karena's mouth, and Noreen smiled.

"You girls are so ambitious and courageous. You get that from your daddy."

"We get a lot of our traits from you, too, Mama," Karena felt compelled to say. She didn't know if it was because taking after Paul Lakefield gave her an unsettling feeling sometimes or if it was that taking after her mother had been the very thing that scared her away from relationships.

"Sometimes I wish I could be that way. Ambitious and courageous."

"But you are courageous. You left your home and your family in South Carolina to be with the man you loved, and you built a great family. That takes courage."

Shaking fingers fixed an already perfect curl just above Noreen's ear. "That's what I was raised to do. From the time I was old enough to see over the sink, my mama had me cooking, cleaning, sewing, taking care of my younger sisters. There wasn't a task at the Big House I didn't do."

The Big House… Karena couldn't help but smile. That's what the sprawling colonial estate in Beaufort, South Carolina, where her grandparents had raised all six of their children was called. And it was a big house. It looked just like Tara, the house Scarlett O'Hara lived in in *Gone With The Wind*. Karena remembered visiting for summers as a child and pretending she, too, wore those big fancy dresses and went to fabulous parties where some dashing man like Rhett Butler would sweep her off her feet.

Of course, the true history of the movie was a slight deterrent, considering the only way she would have been going to fabulous parties in Scarlett O'Hara's time was if she donned a uniform and worked right alongside Mamie. Still, that's the old Southern appeal the Big House held.

"Mama ran that house with no nonsense and a strict hand. She took care of Daddy and raised me to do the same." Noreen sighed. "I had a good teacher and I learned well."

"You're a great mother and wife," Karena said, feeling the need to validate her mother on some level.

Noreen chuckled. "And that's all."

There was so much Karena wanted to say, so many times she'd wanted to have this very conversation with her mother, but now that the time was here, she was speechless.

"I've been thinking about the foundation," Noreen said after taking a deep breath. "About some of the things we could do, really important things."

Karena nodded. "The scholarship fund Uncle Leonard instituted is working well. And I think there's some talk of a new school in Africa." She didn't know much about the foundation's business because the gallery was her world. But as a Lakefield she received the quarterly reports and made a point to read them all. Her father expected nothing less.

"I want to do something with the children, something a little more hands-on."

Karena couldn't believe her ears. Was this really her mother talking?

"That's great, Mama. I'm sure there's a lot you could do. Have you gotten a committee together yet? Had some preliminary strategic-planning sessions?"

Noreen held up a hand, a smile spreading across her face, even though her eyes still looked worried. "No. No. You're moving too fast. I don't have any experience in this kind of stuff, so I have to take my time. I've just been thinking about some things, that's all."

"Well, you have the resources, so there's really no reason why you can't get right to work on this," Karena insisted.

"There sure is a reason," Noreen said seriously. "And his name is Paul Lakefield."

And there it was, Karena thought, the rain on her mother's parade. How a woman could be so in love with a man that she gave him everything she was so totally and unabashedly was a mystery to her.

"He has his work, Mama. Now you can have yours," she said through clenched teeth. There were certain things her mother just did not tolerate, and on top of that list was disrespecting Paul Lakefield. In accordance with her Southern upbringing, Noreen was a strong believer of the man being the head of the household, the ruler of his castle, the leader of their flock. Karena thought he was just a man who put his pants on one leg at a time just like she did. Clearly she'd skipped the lessons on Southern gentility and all that other female-submission nonsense.

"You know your daddy likes things a certain way. He doesn't do change very well."

"He's a big boy, he'll adapt."

Noreen's quick, cool glare had Karena's mouth clamping shut.

"Anyway, I just came to check on you and to see if you wanted to have lunch or something."

What Karena wanted was to finish this conversation. "You've taken care of Daddy for years, Mama. You've taken care of all of us. Now it's time for you. If you want to go to work, then do it. Don't let him stop you. Hell, he can iron his own drawers!"

Noreen was up out of her chair instantly, leaning over the desk until she was only inches away from Karena's face.

She knew she'd overstepped her bounds, but the words had been out before she'd had a moment to think. As grown as she was, Karena's heart still hammered in her chest in anticipation of what her mother would do or say.

In their house sassiness either earned one quick backhanded slap or two days of solitary kitchen duty, depending on how bad the words were. She didn't live with her parents anymore, but still Noreen was looking at her as if that slap was just seconds away.

"You know you aren't too old to be disciplined."

Yeah, she was definitely thinking about slapping her. "I'm sorry, Mama. I didn't mean to say all that."

"You should be sorry. Show some respect."

"I do respect you, Mama," Karena said, standing. "I just think it's time you started standing up for yourself."

"I mean show your father some respect, and I stand up for myself just fine. You don't see him abusing me do you? Am I wanting for anything? My life has been just fine. I could be stuck raising four grandkids like my sister Etta. Or I could be with a husband who drinks his paycheck before the ink is dry on it like my other sister Bernice. But no, your father is a good man, a good provider."

A good dictator, Karena thought but wisely did not say.

"Yes, ma'am," she said instead.

"So I just had some thoughts running through my mind,

they don't really mean anything. Now, do you want to get some lunch or not?"

Did she want to have lunch with her mother? Did she want to sit across the table from the woman she'd watched do everything but spoon-feed her husband his dinner and who now had aspirations of her own but refused to follow up on them because of said man? Hell no!

"I'm kind of busy today, Mama. Maybe some other time."

Noreen had straightened and was already picking up her purse. "You work too hard, Karena. Take some time to smell the roses," she said as she moved to the door. "Before they're old and shriveled, take time to enjoy life. You'll be sorry if you don't."

And as abruptly as she'd come in, Noreen left.

Karena sat back in her chair, wondering just how much her mother was sorry for and if she'd ever do anything about it.

Chapter 10

"Look who decided to pay us a visit today," Sabrina Desdune Bennett said as she leaned back in her chair, legs crossed on top of her desk.

"We were beginning to think you'd forgotten where you worked." This smart remark was from Bailey Donovan, Trent's cousin and Bree's new partner in crime.

Sam eyed both of them. Bree, with her small frame, smooth cocoa skin and long dark hair that was more often than not pulled back into a ponytail, was a petite woman who packed a lot of punch—ask any of the men and women who'd served with her the eight years she was in the Marines. Then there was Bailey, an Alicia Keyes look-alike, dressed in jeans that rode too low on her hips to be legal, a tank top and an open button-down shirt. Bailey was lethal, with brains, beauty and balls bigger than any man walking—a deadly combination on a woman.

Thus his response was carefully worded before it rolled out

of his mouth. Working in the office with two women of this caliber for the past three months had taught him something.

"Good morning, ladies. How's it going?"

When their responses were a mixture of snickers and grunts, Sam kept moving into his office, knowing instinctively that they would follow.

"So why didn't you come back to the office yesterday? Did something else happen on the new case?" Bree asked, sticking her hands into her pockets as she stood on the other side of his desk. Bailey had come in as well, perching her hips on the edge of his desk and looking over her shoulder at him.

"Nothing else happened on the case. Where's the file on Leandro?"

"On my desk," Bree said.

"The Lakefields are very attractive women. How do you know them and which one of them called you?" This was Bailey in her low, smoky voice.

"D&D Investigations is well-known," Sam responded tightly. He didn't like the way they were looking at him, or interrogating him, for that matter. "Don't you have something to do? Follow up on the Chester case maybe?"

"All my leads have run into a dead end. I'm tapping the phones for a ransom call but not really holding out on it. I think it's someone they know who has the girl. Someone they pissed off, looking into possible cartel connections."

Sam looked up from the messages he'd been flipping through as he sat down behind his desk. "Cartel? Are you serious? A drug cartel in Greenwich?"

Bailey shrugged. "Hey, people are getting high all over the world, it's not a segregated pastime."

"Don't be smart. I'm just saying that even during the years I was on the police force, there was never any word of a drug cartel in town."

"You were a suit-wearing homicide detective, of course

you wouldn't know about a cartel," Bree said with more than a hint of sarcasm.

"And you were traveling the world in a uniform with rifles in hand, so don't act like you knew," he shot back at her.

"At any rate," Bailey interrupted, "we all know now that there's a distinct possibility that the Chesters of Greenwich are connected to a cartel in Columbia. When I was out there day before yesterday, I picked up a packet I spotted in the bushes. It had three dots on it, red, black and purple. Agent Greer looked into it for me. It's the mark of the Sanchez Cartel."

Sam was rubbing his chin, digesting Bailey's words. "Sanchez Cartel. So what's your theory on why they took the girl?"

"Revenge. Bad debt. Warning. Punishment. Any number of weird sadistic things that somebody needs to pay for. Greer is working the profiles."

"You sound like you're seeing a lot of Agent Greer. I thought you were told to steer clear of the FBI."

Bailey lifted from the desk and turned, flattening her palms on the desk, her face only inches from Sam's. "Look, you're not my handler and Trent isn't my father. If I want to work for the FBI, then I will and you can't stop me."

Sam nodded. "I can't, but Trent can, and he is." When she was about to go off again, Sam held up a hand. "But that's an argument for another day. Keep working the Chesters and the cartel angle. I want a daily report on where you stand with that. Unfortunately, it's probably a good idea to keep the Feds in on it. Now, Bree, I visited a couple of other galleries that Leandro is showing at. Nothing as high-class as the Lakefield, so he's definitely moving up in the world by contacting them."

"Did you show her the picture? Was it him?" Bree asked.

"No. It wasn't him."

"And that's why you're so uptight?"

"I'm not uptight."

"You are."

"Bree, I'm not in the mood for this today."

"That's because you're uptight. So why don't you just tell us what's eating you so we can get to the bottom of it and move on."

It was times like this Sam hated being a twin. Although he and Sabrina didn't look alike, except for the color and shape of their eyes, they were as close as if they were identical. Something about a twin-sense they shared. And because Bailey was a twin as well, she'd known exactly what they were going through.

"It's just something about the case that's bugging me."

"Something or someone?" Bree insisted.

Sam frowned.

"You never said which sister called you," Bailey said. "They're all intriguing. I researched them last night. There's Monica, the ice queen with an off-the-charts IQ. Then there's Deena, the free spirit with an artistic streak of her own. But I'm putting my money on Karena. The middle daughter with excellent taste in art."

Bailey was too damned thorough. The FBI would be lucky to have her on its side.

"All right, yes, it was Karena who called me. And she called me because we met a few months back at the opening of Linc's new casino. Actually, we met about a month before that. But anyway, she's not the problem." And he was telling the truth in that regard. Karena was not a problem because he knew exactly how he was going to deal with her.

"If she's not the problem then something connected to her and this case is."

"I don't like the vibes I got from the family meeting yesterday, that's all. It's probably nothing. I mean, I know how family can be."

"Oh, yeah, that reminds me, Dad wants us all at the restaurant on Sunday for brunch. He has an announcement to make."

Sam nodded just as his cell phone rang.

"Desdune."

"Hi. It's Karena."

She sounded breathless. Stressed. Worried. He was instantly on alert.

"What's wrong?"

"Nothing. I mean…" she sighed. "I just wanted to see if you'd made any progress."

"No. I'm going over some things with Bree and Bailey now."

"Oh. Okay. Well, call me back as soon as you hear something."

"Are you sure you're okay? If there's something…" Sam stopped, noting the curious gazes of Bree and Bailey as he spoke. He cleared his throat and rephrased his words, because he was definitely getting ready to say if there was something wrong he'd be in Manhattan within the hour. Instead he said, "If there's something you need to tell me about the case, we can schedule a meeting. I'm free this afternoon."

"No. No. That's okay. I don't want to see… I mean, I don't need to…" Again she sighed then took a deep breath. "It's fine. Just give me a call with any updates."

Too late, he thought, he was definitely heading into the city today, just as soon as he could manage it. Something was going on with her. She sounded upset, almost unsure of herself, and he wanted to know why. Had her father been in her office and upset her? Her sister? He felt his protective instincts going into overdrive.

"Sure. I'll call you as soon as I hear something." He disconnected the call because he wasn't alone and free to push her further. And he definitely didn't want to give Bree and Bailey any more tidbits of conversation to speculate over.

"So you want to tell us the truth about what's going on between you and Karena Lakefield now, or do we have to use our superior private-investigator skills to find out on our own?" Bree asked as Bailey gave him a knowing smile.

Sam frowned then shooed them both out of his office. "I'm not paying you to investigate me or my personal life. So get back to work."

Chapter 11

He'd spent the duration of the day worried about her. Sure it was probably foolish. She was a grown woman, she'd made it this long in life without his interference, so if there was something going on with her, she most likely didn't need him now.

But all the rationalizing in the world couldn't keep Sam from climbing into his car and heading back to the city.

There was just something in her voice that bothered him, and he knew he wasn't going to be satisfied with her answer that she was fine until he'd seen it for himself.

Astrid only smiled as he walked through the doors of the Lakefield Gallery once more. He didn't have to ask if Karena was in, he simply walked in the direction of her office.

Lifting a hand, he knocked lightly and waited for her answer.

Seeing her again was like a sucker punch to the gut. She wore a smoky-gray color today. She was sitting behind her desk, so he couldn't see if this outfit was as short as the one she'd worn yesterday. But he knew instinctively it would be just as sexy.

There wasn't a hair out of place and her makeup—although he wasn't usually an expert in this area—added a sensual allure to her. The color of her eyes matched her dress, and the color smudging her lips was much darker than her light complexion but complementary just the same.

Sam realized he could stand there for hours just looking at her, absorbing all the physical traits he was beginning to adore about her. But as she looked up at him, as his gaze locked on hers, the physical attraction abruptly paused.

The worried, stressed vibes he'd gotten over the phone were magnified a million times. He saw it in her eyes and resting on her shoulders like an invisible weight.

"Hey," he said, trying for casual when he really wanted nothing more than to skirt around that desk and grab her up into his arms.

Something told him she wouldn't take too kindly to that.

"Have you heard something?" she asked immediately, dropping the magnifying glass she'd been using to look at some pictures on her desk.

Sam closed the door behind him and compromised from simply scooping her up by moving around her desk and perching himself on the edge. Looking down at her he said, "Have you been worrying over this case all night? Or did something else keep you up?"

Karena sighed, sat back in her chair and frowned. "Don't flatter yourself, Desdune. Last night was good, but I'm no stranger to orgasms."

He chuckled, happy that her quick wit hadn't diminished under the heavy lines of worry marring her forehead.

"I didn't think you were, since you're so well prepared," he said, remembering the way her body had shivered the moment he touched the vibrator to her skin.

It was a dress, he saw the moment he tore his gaze from her face. And it was short. The lower half of her thighs and her knees were visible from where he was sitting, and his body heated instantly.

"A woman has to take care of herself," she quipped.

"Sometimes," he conceded. "But then a man can make the experience so much more rewarding." He reached out then, because he couldn't resist another second, and traced the line of her jaw.

"As long as the end result is the same, I'm inclined to take what I can get."

Her voice was thicker, her eyes just a little cloudy as he touched her. Sam was pleased.

Karena Lakefield was no pushover, nor was she a simpering female who played the game of seduction like a skilled actress. She said and did exactly what she wanted, when she wanted. Problem was, she wanted so desperately to believe that she didn't want it with him. He was going to have a great time proving her wrong.

"Tell me what's really on your mind, Karena. I know it's not what happened between us last night. Is it just the painting? Or is there something else bothering you?"

She opened her mouth to answer, and he put a finger close to her lips to quiet her. "And don't even bother lying. You already know I can see right through that."

He did, she reluctantly admitted to herself. It was uncanny the way he could seemingly see right through her. So the effort of lying or dodging his question was more than fruitless.

"I've got a lot of things on my mind today," she answered.

He nodded. "For instance?"

"What are you, my confidant now?"

"For now, I'll take the title of friend." He was back to touching her face again. "But I plan to change that soon."

"You are so damned arrogant."

He smiled. "You like it."

And because he was right, again, she had no other choice but to muster up a smile in return. "If you say so. Look, there are some family things bothering me and then this painting."

"I see," he said, nodding. "Is it your father?"

"No, thank goodness, he hasn't paid me a visit today. But my mother did and that rattled me. Then I got an e-mail from Monica about an upcoming exhibit. There's just a lot going on."

"What did your mother say that rattled you?"

She moved away slightly, just enough so that he was no longer touching her. "Nothing. It's no big deal. I'm probably just overreacting again."

Were those her words or someone else's?

"Overreacting about what?"

"Look, I appreciate your trying to lend an ear, but I'm fine."

"What you are is too intelligent to believe I'd let you get away with that half-assed answer. But," he said when she looked as if she was ready to argue with him, "since you're clearly not in the mood to talk about what's bothering you, I have a better idea."

Her lips quirked a bit at the ends, making her look surly and suspicious, which for some reason still warmed his blood.

"Let me take you away from all this."

Her forehead creased again. "What? Take me away from what?"

"From whatever is bothering you. Look, you don't have to tell me what it is right now. I'll wait until you're ready. But it's obvious that something is on your mind, and while it is you're not going to get any work done anyway. So, it's Friday, it's four o'clock, we can get out of here, go someplace where you don't have to worry about your mother's words that rattled you. Or your sister's e-mails demanding more of your time. Or this painting situation that I already told you I would handle. You could simply relax."

She chuckled. "No, that's out of the question. I have too much to do."

"And that's why your forehead is beginning to look like a road map from frowning and stressing."

Her hand immediately went to her forehead. "What is it with people staring at my forehead today?"

Sam only lifted a brow. "Stress isn't healthy, Karena. Sometimes you just need a break. I'm offering you that, just for the weekend. Come away with me and let me help you unwind."

He must have truly lost his mind if he thought being alone with him was going to relax her. Karena's mind whirled trying to wrap itself around his offer and the true reasons behind it.

"Will this getaway end with us in bed together?"

"Karena," he said, moving closer to her once more, using his finger to tip her chin up so that she was staring at him eye to eye, "whether we stay here in this office, go back to your apartment or stand at the top of the Empire State Building, we're going to end up sleeping together. That's an irrefutable fact, not a deal breaker."

Sam Desdune was cocky. He was arrogant, pushy, over-bearing and…sexy as hell as he stepped off the elevator with her and walked down the hallway to her apartment.

Because Karena wasn't one to beat a dead horse, convincing her to go away with him this weekend had taken no longer than half an hour. The two subsequent e-mails she received from Monica while he was in her office sort of clenched the deal, too, but that was more like the icing on the cake.

The minute he offered to take her away from all her worries, Karena's heart had soared. Never before had anyone cared that much about what she was going through to offer a solution. Her family just assumed she always had it together, that she didn't need anyone's help, ever. That was most likely due to her fierce independent streak. Still, it seemed that if Sam could see she was nearing the end of her rope, why couldn't the people who were closest to her? She didn't want to entertain the thought that perhaps they did see but chose to ignore it instead of offering her help.

Once inside her apartment, she paused and had a second's hesitation. Did she really know Sam well enough to run off with him? Sure she'd met him months ago, and she knew that if the Donovans and Noelle trusted him so implicitly he had to be a good guy. The fact that he could probably kiss her into an orgasm only added more brownie points. But shouldn't she at least tell her family where she was going, who she would be with, just in case?

Before she could decide, she felt his strong arm wrapping around her waist. How did he do that? How did one touch instantly calm her and wrap her in such a web of security that she simply melted into it?

"You're overthinking this. It's really simple. Pack a bag, come out to my place with me for the weekend where all you'll have to do is eat, sleep and occasionally allow me to touch you. It's not rocket science nor is it your next big business deal."

Both his arms had snaked around her now, her head lulled back to rest against his chest and he'd leaned over so that the warmth of his breath brushed against her ear as he spoke.

Finally she nodded and peeled herself away from him. "I'll just be a few minutes," she told him, moving toward her bedroom.

"Take your time."

She didn't plan on taking that little piece of advice, because as he'd just said she was already thinking this situation to death. In a few more minutes she'd be liable to change her mind.

So the moment she hit her bedroom she picked up her phone and dialed.

"Time is money, money is time. Speak to me."

Karena frowned at the familiar voice who answered. "I really wish you'd stop answering your phone like that, Deena," she said with exasperation. She'd tucked the phone between her ear and her shoulder as she opened her closest door and pulled her overnight bag from the corner.

"Hey, K, what's up?"

Clearly Deena had no intention of discussing her phone-answering skills with Karena. "What if your agent was the one on the phone and you answered that unprofessionally?"

"One, I don't have an agent yet. And two, have you ever heard of caller ID?"

Karena rolled her eyes and moved to her dresser. "Whatever. A simple hello would do nicely."

"Great, when I call you I expect you to answer *your* phone that way."

Sighing, Karena figured it was best to give it up. "Look, I'm heading out for the weekend, just wanted to touch base with someone in case you need me."

"Another business trip? Didn't you just get home? You really need to get a life outside of that gallery, K. I mean, damn, there's more to this world besides temperamental artists and paintings of who really knows what."

"Stop the lecture, I'm not going away on business." Undecided on sleepwear, Karena tossed in two nightshirts and one silky negligee.

"What?" Deena exaggerated the word so that she sounded

more like a teenager on one of those Disney Channel shows than the twenty-seven-year-old woman she was. "You're going on a personal trip?"

"Yes, I am. And before you ask, yes, it's with a man. His name is Sam Desdune. He owns D&D Investigations and lives in Connecticut. That's where we'll be staying. His family owns those restaurants, Lucien's. You know, the one you like in Harlem."

"Oh, yeah, great king cake. Hey, you think you can get the recipe from him? I mean, since you're sleeping with him and all?"

Karena stopped instantly. "I did not say I'm sleeping with him."

"Well, you're spending the weekend with him, that means sex."

"It does not. I just need a break. A change of scenery will be helpful."

"And so will sex, especially if it's good. So take your break, indulge in that change of scenery and get your freak on! Text me to let me know you got there safely and call me with all the details when you get home. Love ya! Smooches!"

And just like that, Deena disconnected the call.

All Karena could do was smile. What she wouldn't give to be that cheerful and carefree for just one day.

Chapter 12

The smooth lyrics of Babyface echoed throughout the car's interior as Karena drove behind Sam's metallic Lexus GS Hybrid. Taking her own car was the smart thing to do, not part of her quest for independence, she'd convinced herself.

Sam had only shrugged when she insisted, giving her that look that was becoming all too familiar to her. So many things about this man were becoming familiar. She'd known him for a little over three months, she'd kissed him and he'd kissed her, right to an orgasm. Were they dating?

Turning off the interstate into what she could only surmise was a small-town setting, her fingers grew lax on the steering wheel, her mind opening to the thought of Sam Desdune without all her usual questions and obstacles.

She could date a man like Sam. Dinners with him would always be filled with lively conversation. Nights in bed with him would certainly be long and satisfying. He was a great listener, if she'd ever open up and really talk to him. The fact that he wanted her to was what scared her.

Who was she kidding? Everything about him scared her because it was all too good. He was too good. Giving herself to him completely would be too easy. Losing herself would be inevitable.

He made a left turn down what looked to be a dirt road. She followed, her breath catching as she noticed the tall trees flanking the roadway. Like a burst of color, orange-and-yellow and muted green leaves decorated the scene. Gone were the honking horns and rushing citizens on the sidewalk, all to be replaced by grassy hills and the sun setting amongst a crimson pillow of clouds.

On impulse she rolled her window down, inhaling the fresh air that did not smell of exhaust or hot dogs and all their gooey toppings like the city she drove through every day. She sighed, letting the change lull her as her car continued to follow Sam's.

Parking in the driveway behind him, she couldn't wait to step out of the car. Words didn't come quickly, which was new for her. She was a salesperson, so talking was part of her trade. She viewed great pieces of art, examined them, sold them, on a daily basis, so this picturesque house and its adorable backdrop should not have held her speechless.

Yet it did.

A split-level ranch was her first impression of his house, but then it wasn't really that simple. The house itself was flanked by more trees, including a huge weeping willow that almost covered what she assumed was the front door. Gorgeous bursts of color came from fall mums in shades of gold, bright yellow and gorgeous plum. The walkway leading to the house was a rock path that continued onto the steps and the small front porch.

But just beyond the house was a creek, looking as if all

Sam had to do was open a window and jump in. A waterfront haven, that's what she'd finally decided this was. Overhead, birds flew by as if welcoming her to their turf. And Sam, who had probably stepped out of his vehicle minutes ago, stood beside her, his hands tucked into his pockets.

"So? Finished with your assessment?" he said, a small smile tilting the edge of his lips.

Karena lifted a hand, pulled her sunglasses from her eyes and turned to him. "It's beautiful. No wonder you hate the city."

"I don't hate the city. I hate driving in the city. Open your trunk so I can get your bag."

She wasn't ready to end her survey, so she handed him the keys she'd taken out of the ignition and fairly ignored him as he moved around her to the back of the car.

"Come on," she heard him say, one hand going around her waist while the other held her duffel bag. "I'll give you a complete tour after dinner."

She nodded and followed him up the path to the door.

He'd just put his key in, turned it and pushed the door open, stepping aside so she could walk in ahead of him, when she was accosted.

The air was knocked out of her lungs in a whoosh as her back slammed against the wall. Before she could form her lips to scream or curse someone out, a warm, wet tongue made contact with her bare shoulder then her neck.

"No! Romeo, down!" she heard Sam yelling from somewhere close by.

Trying to gain her focus, all she could see was a huge head and big chocolate-brown eyes. Huge floppy ears that looked almost cartoonish flapped around the eyes, and she found herself smiling even as Sam pulled the dog away.

"Sorry," he said as he looked up at her, still holding the

dog, who was dancing around trying to get close to her again, by the collar. "His manners suck."

Before she could stop herself, Karena was falling to her knees, dropping her purse to the floor beside her and reaching up to touch those adorable ears.

"Hey, cutie. It's okay. I surprised you, didn't I?"

Yelps of delight vibrated through the foyer as she continued to rub behind the dog's ears. "You're beautiful, aren't you? Look at you." She was rubbing his smooth coat, marveling at the dark gray, almost blue coloring.

"He's a boy, so I'm going to go with he's handsome," Sam told her. "Karena Lakefield, meet Romeo. Romeo, this is Karena. She's not as big as you, so you're not allowed to jump on her."

Karena tossed him a frown then leaned in, snuggling Romeo's large head against her cheek. "He's more than handsome, aren't you, Romeo?"

"I take it you like dogs," he said, unable to hide the pleasure in his tone.

"Love 'em," she answered, still focusing on Romeo, her hands moving over his long back and underbelly. "Daddy wouldn't let us have one in the house, so I had to make do with the ones my friends had."

A pet was probably only one thing in a long list of what Karena Lakefield had been denied, he thought sadly. "Oh, God, now you're going to spoil him."

"Well, he should be spoiled, shouldn't you, boy?"

From his distance above her and the dog, Sam could do nothing but stare. When she'd stepped out of her car, he'd immediately seen the change in her. It was in the set of her shoulders, the relaxation in her stance as she looked around his property. Then when she'd removed her shades, he'd noted the look of sheer wonder in her eyes, the longing for contentment.

Now, here, in the middle of his foyer with his big oof of a dog, she was on her knees laughing and cooing like a child on a hot summer afternoon.

Something inside him warmed and he smiled. "Come on, we can get started on dinner," he said, moving toward the kitchen.

Behind him he could hear her still talking to Romeo as they followed him.

"I don't have much because I wasn't expecting company, but I've got stuff for salad," he said, taking a head of lettuce and some veggies from the refrigerator then moving to the cabinets. "And makings for spaghetti. Will that work?"

Karena had stood, a hand still patting Romeo's head as she looked around. "Spaghetti's fine. If you can cook."

The kitchen was fabulous. Large and airy with marble-tiled floors and countertops. Dark oak cabinets, stainless-steel appliances and flowers. Yes, flowers. Here she was in the midst of a man's kitchen, and her gaze had landed on a clear bowl overflowing with wildflowers.

"I can cook, my family's in the restaurant business, remember. And I like simple things like flowers and big goofy dogs. I see you're surprised by both."

Not even shocked that he knew what she was thinking, Karena moved to the sink and switched on the water to wash her hands. "Well, I can cook, too. So we'll make dinner together. And for the record," she added with a sigh, "I like the simple things, too. I just don't get enough time to enjoy them."

Sam walked to her then touched his lips to hers softly. "Make the time. Life's too short."

His words were too similar to her mother's, and her eyes fluttered closed with the memory. Her lips reacted on their own, seeking his again, sighing as his tongue stroked their plumpness before settling inside.

Life was too short—her mind turned over the words—too short to miss out on kisses like this.

Dinner had been lovely. They'd even cleaned the kitchen together, a feeling that was a little too homey for Karena, but she'd survived.

Now they were sitting on Sam's back porch, the dark sky and humid air surrounding them. Even though it was October, most of the Northeastern states had been experiencing what they called an Indian summer. Luckily she'd changed into a thin cotton sundress before they ate, so the humidity wasn't bothering her too much. Sturdy cushioned porch furniture sat across from an outdoor fireplace and end tables holding more potted plants and various dog toys. Sam's house was large, too large for a single man, but decorated simply with a rustic appeal that touched her.

He looked comfortable in the sweatpants and loose-fitting T-shirt he'd changed into. His feet were bare in thick leather sandals. Now they both sat on a lounge chair that was probably meant for one but held both their bodies snuggly without qualm.

This moment seemed so peaceful, so very right, Karena wanted to fight against it, but was near lost. At the bottom of the two steps which led from the porch, Romeo lay stretched out, resting after the walk they'd taken him for and his own dinner he'd consumed.

From the outside looking in it would appear they were a family, two adults and a dog, living in this fantastic home on this serene piece of land, unwinding from their workweek. Her heart beat a little faster at the thought, and she was about to lift up when Sam's arm went around her shoulders, the fingers of his free hand cupping her chin so that she now faced him.

"But soft, what light through yonder window breaks? It is the east, and Karena is the sun."

With a thud her heart landed, and she feared it was now beating directly at Sam Desdune's feet. "I don't think that's how the quote goes."

Sam shrugged. "I like it better that way."

She was already shaking her head. "We aren't star-crossed lovers."

"No, but we're something. I can feel it and I know you can, too."

"Sam," she whispered, wanting desperately to untwine this web of romantic bliss that seemed to have cocooned them. He was quoting Shakespeare, for goodness' sake, and she was loving the way the words rolled off his lips, reaching out to touch her heart.

His lips touched hers again, this time not as gently as they had before. It was a rough taking, a plea, a request, a demand as his tongue thrust past her lips, twirling and twining with hers.

Karena was helpless to his assault and melted beneath his touch. His fingers grazed her neck, moving down to cup her aching breast. She sighed, lifting a hand to his wrist then covering his fingers, showing him exactly how she wanted to be gripped.

Sam groaned, loving the feel of her plump breast in his hand. Shifting until he was half on top of her, he deepened the kiss while pushing her short dress upward.

"I need to touch you. Feel you," he heard his own guttural voice say.

She was lifting her hips, allowing him to tug her underwear down and off. He didn't wait a moment before thrusting his fingers between her moistened folds the same way his tongue was now thrusting between her lips.

Again the rush of an orgasm was shaking Karena's body.

Yet this time the touch was more intense, more intimate than even before. She lay her head back when his mouth moved from her lips to her neck to take a puckered cotton-covered nipple between his teeth. The second his teeth clamped down, two fingers stroked along the silken walls of her center and a ragged cry fell from her lips. Karena erupted, her release taking her like a fierce, roaring wave.

Sam stood abruptly, pulling his shirt quickly from his chest then stepping out of his shoes and sweatpants. He'd dug into one of the side pockets of his pants before tossing them aside. The sound of the condom package ripping drew her gaze to his groin as he slid the latex on. Watching his fingers glide over his thick arousal had her mouth watering. He groaned and she tore her eyes away from his sex to look at his face. Seeing the intent in his eyes and knowing that this moment was like he said, inevitable, Karena pulled at the hem of her dress, removed it and lay back on the lounge chair.

"I've wanted you for so long," Sam growled, lifting each of her legs and draping them over the arms of the chair.

"We haven't known each other that long." She sighed when his tongue stroked a line along her jaw.

"Too long for us not to have done this before," he replied then settled himself between her legs. "Too long to wait another second."

She opened her mouth to speak then swallowed the words as his thick, heavy length stretched her core, planting him deeply, firmly inside her.

His hands slipped behind her, cupped her buttocks and lifted her to meet his thrusting hips.

"But I've got you now," he was growling in her ear, biting and suckling on her lobe intermittently. "I've got you now."

"It is too rash," she began through panted breaths. "Too unadvised, too sudden."

"Karena," Sam moaned, his hips rocking against hers, pulling out his length then sinking it deep inside once more.

"Too like the lightning, which doth cease to be." Her voice grew louder as the crescendo of yet another orgasm began to ripple through her, the words of Shakespeare falling seamlessly from her lips.

"No, baby. It's not too quick. It's fate. It's meant to be." Sam lifted above her. "Look at me, Karena."

She did, using most of her strength to open her eyes as her hands gripped the muscled splendor of his skin.

"You and me. Here and now, it's just you and me. No doubts and no regrets. Understand?"

She nodded in agreement.

He pulled out until only the tip of his erection touched her weeping center.

"Sam, please," she begged, lifting her hips in an effort to bring him back.

"Say it. Tell me it's just you and me," he said, still holding himself away from her.

It was hard, one of the most difficult things he'd ever had to endure, but Sam did it. Because this was too important, this linking of theirs too serious to let her believe it was just about sex. It wasn't. He'd known it the moment he'd touched her in her apartment. Was it love? He didn't know that much yet. But if it was, he wasn't afraid.

Sam was the type of man who knew what he wanted and went after it full speed ahead.

Right now, however, he needed to hear her admittance, her acquiescence that they were together, or so help him God he was going to die a slow torturous death—or at the very least have an erection for longer than humanly advisable.

"Please, Karena, say it."

"Just…you," she whispered then gained some leverage and

pushed her hips upward just enough so that another inch of his length slid inside her. "And…me."

Sam closed his eyes, groaned. "Yeah," he murmured and let his hips move with hers. She was pumping vigorously against him now, so much so that he could probably remain perfectly still and rush to the finish line well before her.

With that thought he grabbed her hips, kept the deadly weapons still as he pushed himself deep. "You and me."

Then words were pointless. Humidity draped their heated skin as Sam worked over her, pushing her, pushing them to the brink of satisfaction then pulling back. Sweat covered their bodies as ecstasy overtook their thoughts.

Karena was losing her mind. Needing him was driving her insane. With a quick and efficient motion she'd wonder how she achieved sometime tomorrow, she had Sam sitting on the chair as she straddled him.

"You know what you want, don't you?" he asked, cupping a breast then taking the tight nipple into his mouth.

"I do," she said, settling down on his erection and feeling herself being stretched beyond normal lengths. God, he was great, his body so virile and addictive.

"Then take it, baby. Take everything you need."

With his permission, Karena rode him until her head was hanging back, her screams so loud she was thankful for the solitude of Sam's house. Close by she heard the splash and ripple of the creek, felt her own desire rushing in heavy waves through her body.

They came together, Sam clenching her to his chest, Karena's head falling to his shoulder. Their hearts hammered wildly as if trying to break free of their chests to get closer.

"I see you're a fan of *Romeo and Juliet,* too," he said when his breathing was a bit more stable.

Karena smiled, lifting her head to look down into his handsome face. "It's my favorite of Shakespeare's plays."

"Mine, too," he said, taking her lips for yet another scorching kiss.

Sam was standing now, Karena in his arms, her legs wrapped around his waist as he walked toward the house. "Round two," he whispered as she nodded her agreement and smiled.

Chapter 13

"If I don't achieve then I'm as worthless as he thinks."

"Your father can't possibly think you're worthless."

"Not me, per se, but daughters. I was born with the wrong genitalia, and so I must work harder to be accepted, validated."

"That's a bunch of bull."

"Not in the Lakefield household."

Clenching his teeth, Sam rubbed a hand up and down her arm. They were lying in his bed, sunlight just barely beginning to peak through the blinds. They'd made love all night, intermittently talking and laughing, like long, practiced lovers. If felt so right Sam almost moaned. Instead her words were stoking something inherently protective in him.

"I find it hard to believe that a man as intelligent and successful as Paul Lakefield would take such a Neanderthal approach to his children. He couldn't control the sex of his kids no more than any other man on earth."

"That didn't stop him from wanting sons."

Her head rested on his chest, her fingers absently moving over the light brush of hair on his chest.

"But he got daughters, intelligent daughters who as far as I can see are doing a kick-ass job running his business."

She chuckled and a whoosh of warm breath slid over his skin. He hardened instantly, wondering if he'd ever get enough of this woman.

"He's not a bad man," she started talking again. "At least from my mother's viewpoint. I mean, in retrospect, he's been a good father. He's always provided for us, raised us to be loyal and dependable. And if you let my mother tell it, he's the sun, the moon and the stars."

It was Sam's turn to smile and laugh just a bit. "She loves him, huh? Go figure."

Karena swatted playfully at his arm. "I'm not saying it like that. Of course she loves him, we all do. I just think she loves him too much." She was settling against him more closely, lifting a leg to twine with his, scooting her hips so that her warm, still-moist juncture was against his hip. It wasn't a seductive movement, although his body definitely heated in response. No, it was more of a protective stance, a desire to bury herself, her thoughts, in the closeness of him. As if that in some way might make what she had to say go away.

"She's given him everything," she said quietly.

Sam remained quiet. Waiting.

"Her whole life has been dedicated to being a wife and a mother. Until she doesn't know how to do anything else. And she wants to. I know, I saw it in her eyes yesterday. She wants to do something else, be someone else. But she's afraid. Afraid of what he'll say, if he'll approve. It's such bullshit!"

Now she was fired up, her leg sliding from his as she attempted to roll away. But Sam caught her, letting her fall to her side as he spooned her from behind. "Your mother's life is exactly what she wanted it to be. You can't blame her for that," he whispered against her ear.

"I don't blame her," she said, still squirming to get away from him. "Well, yeah, I do. Why didn't she put her foot down, tell him she wants more? Why does she let him dictate her every move, tell her what kind of woman he wants her to be?"

"Is that what you think he's doing? I mean, have you actually heard him tell her what to do and how to do it?"

She stilled and grew quiet. "No. I've never heard them argue. Not even raise their voices at each other in anger."

"Respect," Sam said, his arms folding comfortably around her. "They respect each other and their place in their children's lives."

"But still she's never worked and I know there'd be things she's good at. She said she wanted to work with the foundation, but then she was afraid. Afraid to try. Afraid of what he would say."

"Is that what she said?"

Karena sighed. "No."

"Then how do you know that's what she's thinking?"

"Because that's just like her. All my life she's taken care of him, ironing his clothes, picking out his ties, going to all the business functions on his arm as if she's some sort of decoration instead of his wife."

"Like his partner. A wife is a husband's partner."

"She's still a woman. She should still be her own woman," she said adamantly.

"And she can be, but you can't dictate what or who that woman will be. Some women are content being just a wife or a wife and a mother. It doesn't make them any less than a woman who goes to the office every day and brings home a six-figure salary."

She shifted, looked back and up at him. "What are you, some type of therapist?"

Sam laughed. "No. I'm just a guy on the outside looking in. And I'm thinking that maybe you're a little too hard on your mother and in turn on yourself."

"I am not," she said defensively, turning her face away from his.

He touched a finger to her chin, moving her face so that she could look at him once more. "You are and it's making you miserable."

"I am not miserable," she said with a slight pout.

She was. On the inside she was suffering because of what she thought her mother's supreme sacrifice was, for what she swore she would not become. In this one night her entire life's dilemma had been laid out for him, and true to his nature Sam felt the overwhelming desire to fix it. To make everything better for her.

But for right now, he knew he wouldn't accomplish that by continuing with this conversation. As they'd lain here she was already beginning to pull away, her body stiffening beneath his gaze and his words.

Only one thing could relax her, could bring her back to the place where he wanted her to be.

With that thought Sam kissed her, brushing his lips over hers lightly as his body shifted until he was on top of her.

"You're a terrific woman, Karena," he whispered between kisses, between swipes of his tongue over her lips. "A beautiful, vibrant woman who's smart and successful."

She was loosening beneath him, her palms going to his chest, her mouth opening to his wordless command.

"You'd be a great wife, a great complement to the right man." To him, his mind roared but smartly remained quiet.

"No," she whispered, shaking her head but snaking her own

tongue out to touch the tip of his. "I don't want to complement a man. I want to live my own life, on my own terms."

With deft precision Sam let his tongue duel with hers, their eyes remaining fixated on each other as they touched. Dipping his head he deepened the connection, thrusting his tongue inside her mouth, pressing her head farther into the pillow.

She sighed and moaned into the kiss, giving him exactly what he wanted. What he sensed was all she thought she could give. If she only knew, Sam thought, with a moan of his own.

It was her turn, Karena realized, and she stretched an arm to his nightstand where he'd wisely left a stack of condoms. She ripped one open and rolled it onto his length, loving the feel of his arousal growing harder, warmer beneath her touch.

Then with his knees he spread her thighs, let his aching erection seek and find the wet warmth it was searching for. When his thick tip touched her entrance, she gasped. He sucked her tongue, pulling it deep into his mouth as his arousal slipped slowly, deeply, inside her sugared walls.

In that instant Karena felt something within her snap. Nothing painful or harmful, but an opening, a breaking through of sorts, speared by this man's dominant entrance into her physically and, unfortunately, emotionally.

He moved over her with a painful slowness, his erection stretching her, opening her, molding her perfectly around him. He lifted her legs, planted the soles of her feet on his chest and pumped inside her deeply, slowly. As if he had all the time in the world to stroke her.

Her eyelids felt heavy with the haze of lust and something not so easily described hovering throughout the room. As the thick slashes of sunlight slipped through the miniblinds at the window, falling over Sam's bronzed naked body and giving him an ethereal look—like a Greek god—Karena felt the first ebbings of fear.

Not the kind that said he would hurt her, use her, leave her. But the kind that told her that inevitably she would do those things to him.

She closed her eyes tightly, trying to shut the truth out of her mind, to concentrate solely on the delicious feel of him. He lifted one leg, held it away from them so that she probably looked like a member of the Olympic gymnastics team with her limbs spread in weird contortions. But the act gave him a different angle, let him sink his erection into her seemingly deeper. Her center oozed with desire, coating them both, the sound echoing, mixing with her slow moans and his guttural groans.

He pulled her leg back to his chest, stroked his tongue over the sole of her foot, stopping to take one toe into his mouth for a French kiss unlike any she'd experienced before.

Karena's body shook uncontrollably. What was he doing to her?

Again Sam shifted until he was sitting in the center of the bed, pulling her on top of him and wrapping her legs around his waist. Their chests were entwined, his thick length sliding upward into her waiting center. He pulled her down on his length slowly, keeping his eyes fixated on hers as he did.

Karena was lost. For now. For this moment, she was simply lost. All inhibitions, arguments, defenses, were gone. As he'd said over and over again throughout the night, it was just him and her.

And for now, for this moment, she would take that. She would take him, she thought, lifting slightly then settling down on his thickness with a contented sigh.

He hugged her to him tightly, almost too tightly, but she didn't mind. She let her forehead fall to his shoulders as their centers thrust and gyrated together. It was so sweet, too torturously good to stop, but she knew she was growing closer.

And as Sam continued those lethal thrusts of his hips, pushing his thickness deeper into her, she let out a tortured moan then found herself biting the taut skin of his shoulder as if she was some bloodthirsty vampire. She moaned, her eyes closing as the sweetest, most intense orgasm ripped through her.

Sam followed immediately, holding her bottom so that his member was glued inside her, his orgasm ripping from him to mingle with her own. He closed his eyes and whispered her name, over and over again as his feelings, emotions, trickled out with his essence, entering her, touching her, whether she wanted them to or not.

Chapter 14

"Um, um, um, you look great in my kitchen," Sam said the moment he walked into the room after taking Romeo for his morning walk.

Karena was at the stove flicking her wrist as she scrambled perfectly fluffy yellow eggs in the skillet. At the sound of his voice she'd jumped only slightly. Inside, however, her defenses were rising.

He was already behind her before she could speak, wrapping his arms around her waist and cuddling to her back. Romeo barked and she looked down at him, patted him on the head then yanked her free hand back.

This was too comfortable, seemed too normal.

She picked up the skillet and moved out of Sam's grasp. "Hungry?" she asked, not looking directly at him.

After he'd left her this morning she'd had time to think. Last night had been good…too good. For a minute she'd believed that she could just fall in love with Sam Desdune. As easily as she'd drifted off to sleep in his arms, she figured she could accomplish that task.

But then what?

What would he expect of her once she admitted he owned her heart? He'd want to own the rest of her, no doubt.

"Starving," he said cheerfully, and she could hear him moving behind her to the large dark oak table sitting in the middle of his spacious kitchen.

She'd already cooked bacon and waffles and was now fixing them both a plate. Plates in hand, she turned and carried them to the table, setting one in front of Sam and the other in front of the high-backed stool for herself.

"You should have gone out walking with us. It's beautiful in the morning. The air's so crisp and refreshing."

Karena nodded. Of course the air here would be perfect, just like the man and the dog that barely had to lift its head to sniff at the food sitting on the counter. Sam gave Romeo a warning glance, and the dog's large head fell downward a few inches. Feeling sorry for him, Karena rubbed Romeo behind the ears before taking her seat.

"I figured I'd cook breakfast to return the favor of your cooking dinner last night."

Sam nodded and reached for her hand.

She was instantly pulling back.

"Let's bless our food then we can eat," he said easily, his dark brown eyes holding her gaze.

Last night he'd blessed their food before they'd eaten, and she'd bowed her head and joined him. At the restaurant, she remembered, he'd done the same. This morning, after their night of lovemaking, was the first time he'd reached for her hand to do so.

Another warning bell sounded in her head, but she felt herself surrendering her hand to his grasp.

He prayed almost like a preacher and her entire body

warmed, not with desire but with a calmness that bordered on complete serenity.

This was insane! He was just a man and they were just having sex. She wasn't falling in love. She couldn't.

"Amen," she heard herself saying, and she almost frowned when Sam released her hand before she could pull away.

Clearing her throat, she decided to keep things as normal and casual as she could. "So what's on your agenda for the day? Do you have to work?"

He shook his head. "No. Bree faxed me some copies of Leandro's artwork because I wanted to get a look at more of the guy's pieces. So far I don't know who the guy you met with was, but we're trying to track him down based on your description."

She nodded. "We'll probably never find him. And I really don't care. I just want to get the paintings back to their rightful owners."

"Where is it now?"

"In our warehouse. I didn't want it on the gallery floor if it isn't legally ours."

"Good idea. We'll find this guy because he owes you money. You paid him well for the portrait, and if it wasn't his to sell then he'll answer for it."

"I just should have known better," she said, looking down at her food. Her father had said as much, and while Monica hadn't echoed his words, Karena knew her always-perfect, ever-efficient sister was thinking it.

"There was no way you could have known. The sad thing is that the guy has probably done this before." With a look of resignation, Sam lifted a piece of bacon from his plate, lowered his arm from the table and let Romeo have a slice.

Again Karena's heart melted for this man. Why couldn't she let herself love him? Why couldn't she just ignore those warning bells and take the plunge?

"You look really good here, Karena. In my house, in my kitchen, you look like you belong," he said, eyeing her seriously, and the breath froze in her lungs.

The answer to her questions had been made so painfully clear in those two sentences.

She cleared her throat. "I belong in Manhattan. That's where I live. It's where my job is."

Sam forked eggs into his mouth and chewed. She tried not to notice the strength in his shoulders as the T-shirt he wore did nothing to hide his great physique. It took even more effort not to watch his mouth as he chewed or notice that his glare was serious, intense and unwavering.

"My job is twenty miles away but I belong here."

He sounded so sure of himself, always. Decisions, goals, achievements, all those things probably came easily to Sam Desdune. But not to her.

"My family's in the city."

"So is mine."

Her fork fell to her plate with a clatter that had Romeo jumping then moving noisily out of the room. "I'm where I want to be."

His left brow lifted. "Today? Right at this moment? Physically or mentally?"

"Don't do this," she said, shaking her head.

"Don't do what?"

"Don't make this more than it has to be."

"You mean don't make it about feelings, just keep it about sex."

Folding her hands in her lap, Karena sat back in her chair and stared at him with the same intensity as he was giving her. Two could play this game. "Yes, let's just keep it about sex."

He was already shaking his head negatively. "That's not what I do."

"That's not my problem."

He chuckled, lifted his napkin to his lips and wiped his mouth. "No. It's not. But I do know what your problem is."

"Oh, please enlighten me," she said sarcastically.

"You're afraid."

"Wrong. I'm not afraid of anything." The words tasted dishonest in her mouth.

"I've said this before, don't make me say it again. We're both too intelligent to try lying."

She wanted to pick up her plate, slam it into the sink and leave his arrogant, sexy ass sitting in the kitchen alone, but she didn't. "Just because I don't want flowery words and bull-crap declarations doesn't make me afraid. It makes me smart enough to know my limitations."

"Limitations you've placed on yourself?"

"Whatever the reason or the origin, they are my limitations and I live by them."

He leaned forward, placing his elbows on the table and resting his chin on steepled hands. "When I first met you in Noelle and Brock's kitchen, I distinctly remember thinking, 'Damn, this woman's got her act together. She's beautiful, successful, intelligent, funny, the total package.' Never once did I figure you for the type to let someone else's choices dictate your life."

Her heart pounded, her cheeks warmed. His words hurt, touched and inflamed all at once. How did he do that? How did he make her so angry she could smack him one minute then have her melting like putty in his hands the next, and vice versa? She had no idea, but her head was beginning to hurt. This wasn't how the morning was supposed to turn out.

"Look," she said, finally giving in to the urge to run by standing and pushing the chair out behind her. "I came here this weekend to get away from the stress of work. I didn't sign up for more issues."

He didn't respond, simply sat back in his chair and stared at her. The silence was just as unnerving as his self-assured declarations. She didn't know what to do with either.

"I'm not going to lie, sex between us is good," she started again then picked up her plate and moved it to the sink. Turning, leaning her bottom against the counter, she folded her arms and continued, "But it's just sex. That's all I want it to be. My reasons are my own and I don't need you analyzing them."

He'd already begun nodding but she could tell by the set of his shoulders he was hardly in agreement with her. "Then what do you need me for? You've got your toys at home to bring you an orgasm. You don't need me to give you advice, you don't want me to analyze you or your immature limitations. So what *do* you need me for?"

The biting edge to his voice was more than she'd expected. However, it did what up until now she hadn't been able to do on her own. It spurred enough anger that she could do what needed to be done. "This was a mistake," she said simply then started out of the room.

He was up so fast she didn't have time to think, grabbing her around her waist and pushing her back against the counter.

"Don't even think it," he whispered hoarsely, his face lowering closer to hers. "Don't even give yourself that pitiful excuse. This wasn't a mistake. Not you coming here, not us sleeping together, not you enjoying every minute of it. It was real. It *is* real and it's more important than anything you've ever had to face in your life."

She tried to squirm out of his hold. It was too much, the heat of his touch, the sting of his words, the betrayal of her heart over her mind.

"You don't want to feel it, fine," he breathed against her lips. "You want to try to ignore it, go right ahead." He bit her bottom lip, licking over the spot when she'd jumped at the pain.

"But don't try to tell me it was a mistake. I know exactly what it was and I know exactly what I feel."

His tongue was warm and thick as it passed over her lips. She didn't want to kiss him, didn't want to open her mouth to the assault of sensations she knew it would bring.

"You feel lust," she said finally.

"You're damned right I do." He groaned as he bent a little at the knees, matched his thick erection with the heated mound between her thighs and pushed. "You feel lust, too."

He was pressing into her so she leaned back, trying to give herself breathing space, thinking room. Sam wasn't trying to hear it.

"But you feel something else. You feel the emotions that are tangled up in the physical. The sensations that whirl around in your mind after I've kissed you. The ache that never seems to go away no matter how many times you come. I know that's what you feel because I feel it, too."

His lips covered hers as they both bent over the counter. "I feel it, too, Karena. And I want more. I need more."

She opened her mouth to speak and lost the words as his tongue snaked inside, sliding along hers before enticing it out to play. This kiss was a desperate tangle of moans and desires. Her palms slammed against his chest as his went to her bottom, gripping her cheeks and pulling them closer together.

It was too much, all of it and just this part of it. Sam and this house and his dog. His words, his touch. The truth, the past, the confusion, everything was just too damned much and Karena wanted to scream.

Instead she tore her lips away from his and pushed him back roughly. He looked stunned, which she was herself since he was so much taller and broader than her.

"I don't need more, Sam. That's what you're going to have to accept. I can do the sex thing and that's fine. But anything else," she said, trying to catch her breath, "it's just not negotiable."

And then because every fiber in her being screamed that she jump on him, wrap her legs around his waist and let him have her once more, she stormed out of the kitchen and headed directly to the bedroom, where she grabbed her purse and overnight bag and left.

Chapter 15

He hadn't stopped her from leaving.

Why?

Because he wasn't in the habit of begging or chasing a woman.

Did he miss her?

Like the night would miss the day, dark would crave the light, right inevitably sought out wrong.

Entering Lucien's of Greenwich he walked straight to the back, the room that was reserved every Sunday morning from eleven to two in the afternoon for the Desdune family brunch.

He hadn't stopped to speak to Cary, the bartender, or Marlese, the host. He'd simply swung open the door and stomped inside. His steps were long, purposeful, his mind not on brunch or family or anything else but her.

She was supposed to be with him. That's what he'd thought

this time yesterday morning when he'd been out walking Romeo and she'd been in his kitchen preparing breakfast.

The whole scene had felt so right, so homey, so everything Sam had ever wanted. The sad thing was, it wasn't enough for him to want it alone.

His cell phone rang a second before he entered the back room. He stopped, pulled it free of the holder on his waist and hoped to see a familiar number.

He got his wish.

Then again, he didn't.

"Desdune," he answered reluctantly.

"Hi, Sam. I've been trying to get in touch with you for days now."

Her voice was sugary sweet, and Sam could just imagine how she looked. It was Sunday morning so she'd be dressed for her appearance at the First Joshua Baptist Church.

Leeza Purdy would be dressed in an impeccable suit, her heels would be high, patent leather probably. She'd have a matching hat on her head, purse in one hand and Bible that didn't open any other day of the week in the other.

"I've been working."

"I figured. You're always working. I keep telling you it's too much," she began.

Yes, she had told him he worked too much. During the year they'd dated she'd told him so many things—complained about so many things was more like it.

"I'm on my way to brunch. Is there something I can do for you, Leeza?"

"Well, yes. I'm calling about the charity ball. Are you wearing your black tux or the white one? Actually, I think this year would be better if you wore the black pants and white dinner jacket."

With his free hand, Sam rubbed his temple and watched as his brother, Cole, stepped up beside him.

"I won't be attending the charity ball this year, Leeza, so it really doesn't matter."

"What? Not attending?" She giggled. "Of course you're going, Sam. It's the most important function of the season. Everybody who is anybody at the club will be there. Your parents will certainly be there and the Bennetts, so it makes sense that you and I attend."

Cole stood close, at least three inches taller than Sam's six-foot-one stature. His older brother had the mocha skin of their mother and sister Bree. His wavy black hair was cut low and matched the dark, expertly trimmed goatee on his face. His thick brows raised in question. Sam frowned, moved his free hand from his temple and twirled one finger around near his head, indicating that Leeza was crazy.

Cole chuckled. The Desdunes as a whole had been extremely happy the day Sam broke off his engagement with Leeza.

"Even if I were going to the ball, Leeza, we wouldn't be going together. Our relationship is over, remember?"

He could hear her pouting over the phone, if that were possible. "Sam, we are not going to have another unsavory scene like the last one."

"No. We're not," Sam said with the last bits of his control wearing extremely thin. "There's no need for a scene, as you put it. The fact is that we aren't a couple anymore. Plain and simple."

"There's nothing plain and simple about this foolishness you keep spreading. I've already had to deal with the rumor mill after you so rudely made your feelings known at the restaurant."

He hadn't thought he was rude. He'd simply had enough. And when he'd decided to tell her that in a nice, calm manner, she'd been the one to go off, yelling and screaming as if he'd slapped her. Which, coincidentally, if he weren't raised to treat women like the queens they were, he probably would have.

"It's done, Leeza. You need to find yourself another date to the ball." And because he was definitely tired of hearing the high-pitched squeal of her voice and had just spotted Bree and her husband, Renny, coming through the front door of the restaurant, he disconnected the phone.

"Not taking no for an answer, huh?" Cole asked as Sam put the phone back into its case.

"You know Leeza, if it's not what she wants to hear, she has trouble accepting it."

"Yeah, I'm just glad you had the good sense to dump that controlling windbag."

Sam frowned at Cole. "Go ahead and tell me what you really think about the woman I was going to marry."

"Hey, the operative word here is 'was,' little bro. Like I said, I'm glad you dumped her when you did. Otherwise we all would have had to endure her loud, whining talk every week at these gatherings."

"Mornin'," Bree said, approaching her brothers and looking suspiciously from one to the other. "What's going on?"

"Nothing," they both said in unison.

Bree arched a brow. Of Cole and Sam and her husband, Renny, who stood behind her, she was the shortest, craning her neck to look up at the men.

"You were talking about something before I approached," she said slowly.

Renny put an arm around her waist. "The fact that they stopped talking about it when you arrived means it has nothing to do with you," he interceded. "What's up Sam? Cole?" He spoke with a nod to each brother.

"Hey, Renny," Cole said, reaching out a hand and shaking his brother-in-law's. "She's still a nosy little spitfire."

Renny chuckled as Bree continued to glare at Sam.

"I don't think that's going to change, no matter how hard we try," Sam said, mimicking Cole's move and shaking Renny's hand.

"She's getting better," Renny said in his wife's defense.

"I can't tell," Sam was saying when a little boy ran up to him, wrapping his arms around his legs.

"Uncle Sammy, Uncle Sammy!" Jeremy Richardson, Sam's five-year-old nephew, looked up at him with the biggest teddy-bear-brown eyes Sam had ever seen.

His bad mood melted instantly.

Bending, Sam scooped the little boy up into his arms. "Hey, little man. How've you been?"

"Good," Jeremy responded as Sam settled him on his hip. "Mama got me a Spider-Man outfit for Halloween."

"Whoa, trick-or-treaters better watch out then, Spider-Man is going to be on the prowl."

"I got a bag and candy in the bowl to give out. I want to eat the Reese's cups, but Mama won't let me."

"That's right, if you start eating them we won't have any left next week to give away." Lynn Desdune with her tall, athletic frame had joined them. She was smiling today, a light in her eyes that Sam hadn't seen in a while and that made him happy.

Lynn had been through a lot, marrying young, having a baby and then her no-good husband just up and leaving her and Jeremy. Earlier this year Sam thought he'd seen something between her and Trent, but that fizzled. And based on Lynn's own words, "It was just sex and it was good." So he hadn't felt the need to pull his longtime friend up about messing with his sister. It seemed as though they were two consenting adults, taking care of their needs. Lynn had actually been pleased to hear about Trent's engagement and expected parenthood.

"So what are you dressing up as?" Sam asked Lynn.

"I was just going to ask you that question, since he wants you to take him trick-or-treating."

"Yeah, can you, Uncle Sammy, can you?"

No way was Sam going to decline. His nephew meant too much to him. Family meant too much to him, which is why he wanted to start one of his own so badly.

Unfortunately, the woman he was now convinced was perfect for him had other ideas. She was of Lynn's "just sex" mentality, and that just wasn't flying with him.

Come hell or high water, Karena Lakefield was going to see things his way.

"So, Sam, tell us about this Karena Lakefield," Marie Desdune asked her son when they were drinking mimosas and sitting around the large banquet table.

Sam shot Bree an irritated glare, and ornery nymph that she was, she only smiled and lifted a brow as if waiting for his response.

"She's a client," he responded in a clipped tone.

Marie nodded her head. She had the same milk-chocolate complexion as Bree and Cole. Her short stature gave her a pleasingly plump appearance, while her jet-black hair was stylishly curled.

"You don't usually take clients to your house," Marie added with an impish smile of her own.

How had they known Karena was at his house? No doubt the newest private investigator in the family had found out that little tidbit of information. Well, he'd been a member of this family long enough to know there was no use in trying to keep anything away from them.

"She needed a break from the job and all the stress of the case, so I brought her out to the house for a relaxing weekend."

"And you didn't bring her to brunch to meet us?" Marie asked.

"She had to go back to the city yesterday."

"Hmm, doesn't seem as if you were successful in helping her relax if she ran back to work so quickly." This was Cole, casting his normal brotherly barbs.

Probably seeing that his son needed saving, Lucien Desdune chimed in. "What's her case about, son?"

Sam breathed a sigh of relief. "Stolen artwork. Some guy impersonated an artist and sold Karena's gallery a stolen painting. Apparently there have been other stolen paintings reported."

Renny, who also owned an art gallery and was a talented sculpture, spoke next. "I've been hearing about a lot of that going on. Have you found the owners of the paintings?"

"Not yet," Sam said. "This artist, Leandro, is reputedly some recluse. We're trying to track him down, since the insurance companies are being really tight-lipped about the owners."

"So a claim has been filed?" Renny asked.

"No," Bree answered. "Not yet. All we have are the appraiser's reports saying that the paintings were stolen. That's why we figure finding Leandro is our best bet for figuring out whom he really sold the paintings to."

Renny nodded. "That's probably a good angle. But it's weird that none of the owners of the paintings have reported them missing yet. I've heard of Leandro. His work is in high demand. If somebody owned one of his pictures, they'd know immediately if it went missing and they'd definitely have it insured."

Sam agreed one hundred percent with what Renny was saying. That had been the part of the case that had puzzled him.

"Sounds like you've got a lot of work ahead of you. Probably not a good time for you to be chasing a client's skirt," Lucien added.

Leave it to his father to be candid. "I'm not chasing her skirt, Dad."

"Nah, if she was at his house he's already achieved that goal," Cole joked.

"Don't be crass," Marie admonished.

"And it's not like that," Sam defended. "Karena's not like that. She's dealing with a lot right now. Her father's really hard on his daughters when it comes to business. I think he'd prefer they all get married and become housewives like his wife."

"But Karena doesn't want that?" Marie asked.

"No. Neither do her two sisters. From what I can tell they're all just as ambitious and stubborn as their father."

"Why is that they are always made to seem like bad traits for a woman?" This was Lynn, Sam's oldest sister, speaking up.

"I didn't say it was bad, just hard to deal with when they all keep butting heads."

Marie took another sip of her mimosa, watching her son carefully. "Well, if anybody can help her, Sam, it's you."

"Yeah, Sam's the hero of the family," Bree said with a smile.

He frowned and would have given another smart remark but a cell phone rang.

"Oh, that's me," Bailey said, quickly pulling out her phone and looking at it. "I've got to go."

"But you barely ate anything," Marie said quickly. Although Bailey wasn't blood-related, the Desdunes were the closest thing she had to family in Greenwich, and with Trent's request that Sam keep an eye on her, the rest of his family had dutifully fallen in step. "You should eat more and slow down. Working is not everything."

"Thanks, Ms. Desdune. But I'm okay, really," Bailey was saying as she slipped her purse strap on her shoulder and went around the table to give Marie a hug. "I'll have a big dinner," she whispered into the older woman's ear.

"Make sure you do. And call me tomorrow so we can talk. You look as though something's bothering you."

Bailey was already shaking her head, her long braids moving with the motion. "I'm fine," she started saying. "But I'll call you anyway."

Marie smiled, appeased with Bailey's acquiescence. Next Bailey hugged Lucien, who looked at her with the same worried expression he gave his daughters. "Be safe," he said.

Bailey kissed his cheek and was on her way out when Sam stopped her.

"What's going on?"

She leaned over and whispered, "I've got a lead on the Chester kid. I'll call you later with the details."

Sam had to agree with Marie and Lucien—Bailey didn't look like she was okay. He'd have to make a point to deal with that.

Chapter 16

Karena walked into her office bright and early Monday morning, determined to put the tumultuous emotions from the weekend out of her mind. She'd spent the latter part of Saturday and all day Sunday in her apartment, trying like hell to ignore the gnawing need for Sam's touch, for the sound of his voice, his laughter and even, heaven help her, for the sight of his gorgeous dog, Romeo.

What a silly name, she thought, sinking into her chair and clicking the buttons to turn her computer on. Who would name their dog after a character in a play, unless it was your favorite play. The tragic story of Romeo and Juliet, star-crossed lovers who would never see the happiness that their hearts so eagerly bled for. Thinking about the story made her sad. No, to tell the truth, thinking about Sam made her sad.

Why did he have to want something she couldn't give? Better yet, why couldn't she give him what he wanted? Too many questions, Karena thought, clicking her mouse in an automatic gesture, opening programs and waiting as her overflowing inbox appeared on the screen.

Sam wanted forever. She'd seen it in his eyes as he'd taken her hand in his and said the grace that would bless their breakfast on Saturday morning. He wanted a family, home and hearth. He wanted to build something—something akin to what his family already had. And truth be told, there was a part of Karena that longed for the same thing. Yet there was an even bigger part that wanted to run like a screaming banshee from it all.

It wasn't in her. It just wasn't.

She wasn't housewife material. Hell, maybe she wasn't even mother material. Who knew? All Karena knew for sure was that her entire life had been steered toward succeeding in business and showing her father that she was just as good, if not better, than any son he could ever have hoped for. As for her mother, there really wasn't anything Karena felt she could prove to her.

Noreen was already set in her ways, in her beliefs of what a mother and wife should be. It had been instilled in her from her Southern-bred childhood, and she'd done an excellent job at it. Why she couldn't have strived for more, Karena had no clue. But she had begun to believe that maybe it wasn't for her to figure out. Maybe her mother's life had been exactly what her mother had wanted it to be.

Her head was beginning to hurt. Stress was a killer. She knew this because she'd read plenty of articles on the subject. Just as she'd felt the warning signs attacking her body. Tension set in her shoulders like heavy bricks while her temples throbbed. She reached into her drawer and pulled out the jar of extra-strength aspirin she'd brought from the wholesale warehouse because five hundred in a bottle just made more sense to her than going to the drugstore and buying a bottle of twenty-five, knowing she'd take those twenty-five in the span of one week.

She hadn't eaten breakfast but she did have a cup of coffee nearby, so she popped two aspirin, took a sip of coffee and reminded herself she needed to get to work. The things going on in her personal life had no place at the gallery. She'd have to deal with them later.

Just as she clicked open the first e-mail from Monica, there was a knock on her door. She looked up and felt the coffee and two pills she'd just swallowed twist and turn in her stomach.

This wasn't going to be good, somehow she knew.

She was the last person he expected to hear from this morning. That's why when he walked into the office and Bree handed him a message from Karena's office, Sam felt momentarily confused.

Saturday had been a roller-coaster ride for them both. Between the heated emotions emanating from their sensuous lovemaking and the surface covering their deeper feelings for each other, they were both going crazy. He'd sensed it and yet he'd pushed anyway. Why? Because that's the way he was. When Sam decided he wanted something or someone, the way he had decided with Karena, he went after it, no holds barred.

Unfortunately, Karena hadn't appreciated that approach.

He moved with slow strides into his office with Bree hot on his heels.

"It was her assistant who called, saying that Karena had some very important people in her office and she needed you to get there as soon as possible," she said with a serious tinge to her tone.

Sam had just dropped his bag onto the chair and turned back to her with what he knew was a frown on his face. "What important people? And why didn't she just call me at home or on my cell?"

"Who? Karena or her assistant?"

He was not in the mood for Bree's questioning right now. Thanks to her, he'd endured the third degree from the family enough yesterday at brunch.

"Who are the people in her office? Does it have to do with the painting?"

"I suppose so because she wants to know if you can come to the city ASAP."

That wasn't even a question. Of course he was going to the city to see what was going on. But first, he wanted to know what he was walking into. So picking up the phone, he hurriedly dialed the number to the gallery.

The phone was answered on the second ring. "Hi, Astrid, this is Sam Desdune, is Karena available?"

"Hi, Sam, no, she's not available. She's been closed in her office with the prince and princess and Monica for over an hour."

"The prince and princess?" Sam was confused.

"Yes. They came in early this morning from Brazil. They want to know how she came across their painting."

"Dammit!" Sam swore. Bree had been tracing the painting but hadn't come across any official ownership information besides the appraisers' reports, almost as if the ownership itself was being kept a secret. "I'll be there inside the hour," he snapped and was about to hang up the phone when another thought hit him. "Astrid, can you tell me the prince's and princess's name or where they're actually from?"

"Sure, I wrote it down," she paused and Sam heard papers shuffling in the background. "Here it is, Felipe and Izabel de Carriero from Pirata."

Sam couldn't help the small smile that ghosted his lips. "Thanks. Get a message to Karena that I'm on my way." He pressed the release button on the phone then grabbed another line and began dialing numbers once more.

"What's going on, Sam? Who are you calling now?" Bree asked.

"Your brother-in-law," he said then quickly asked the person who answered the phone for Alex Bennett while Bree stared at him quizzically.

"Sam, my man, what's got you calling me this early on a Monday morning?" Alex Bennett answered in a voice more jovial than he gave any of his employees.

The oldest brother of the Bennett clan, Alex was determined, authoritative and focused. He loved his family but he probably loved his job as CEO of Bennett Industries even more. Still, when things had gotten sticky with the Bennett stalking, Alex had proved himself as a family man and a force to be reckoned with. And since Bree had married Alex's younger brother, Renny, they'd all seamlessly shifted into the in-law status, sharing lots of family gatherings together.

"Hey, Alex. Sorry to bother you, but I think I have something you might be interested in going on." In addition to being ambitious and determined to run the best damned communications firm on the East Coast, Alex was also dogged about preserving his family's heritage.

"Yeah? What's up?"

"Long story short, I have a client who may have purchased a stolen painting from an artist living in Brazil. This morning a Prince Felipe de Carriero and his wife showed up at my client's office claiming ownership of the painting."

"De Carriero?" Alex asked immediately.

"That's why I called. Can you spare a few hours to head into the city with me? I want to check them out, check out their story because there are too many imposters moving around in this case."

"Sure. No doubt I want to check this out, too. Let me get

my secretary to clear my schedule. I can be at your office in ten minutes and we can ride in together. Or do you just want me to meet you there?"

"Yeah, why don't you just get on the road after you get your schedule squared away. I want to leave right away. Karena shouldn't have to deal with them by herself, and I don't want her father coming in and stirring up more trouble. Call Bree when you're set to leave and she can give you the address and directions."

"No problem."

"Thanks, Alex."

"Don't mention it. See you in a little while."

Sam disconnected and reached for his bag. Bree was on his heels as he headed out of the office.

"So why did you call Alex and where are you going?"

He couldn't not answer her. Besides, he needed her to keep digging into this guy Leandro's history. "The prince and princess of Pirata are in New York. It seems our mysterious painting might be theirs."

"Pirata? That's where Renny's mother is from."

"And that's why I called Alex. If there's a relation between the prince and princess to the Bennetts, he'll know. And that relation might just give us the insight into this case that we need to find out who sold Karena the portrait. So when Alex calls back, give him the directions to the gallery. Then I want you to trace Leandro's family, find out where he comes from, who he knows and how it's connected to the prince and princess, and text me the info."

Bree was already nodding her head.

"Where's Bailey?" Sam asked just as he was about to walk through the door. It was the first time he noticed she wasn't in the office, and Bailey was usually the first one in every morning.

"Don't know." Bree shrugged. "I haven't seen or heard from

her since yesterday when she left the restaurant. I was going to call her a little later if she didn't show up."

Sam didn't like the sound of that. "Call her now and make sure she's all right." Then he was out the door and headed to his car.

Bree could only shake her head as she watched her brother pull out of the parking lot. That was Sam, one of her closest friends besides her husband. Nobody knew him like she did. That's why her heart gave a little flutter as she realized what was happening here. Sam was falling in love with Karena Lakefield, if not already knee-deep in the sticky emotion already.

He was also worried about Bailey, which wasn't a good sign. When Sam worried, there was usually good reason to. And Sam would be determined to fix whatever Bailey's problem was, just as he'd had to fix Bree's problem with the older man who had ruined her military career and tried to take her life. And just as he was going to be the hero and save the day for Karena. It was just what Sam did, and he did it so well Bree couldn't help but be proud of him.

She only hoped this Karena Lakefield knew what a great guy she had falling for her.

Once again walking through the doors of the Lakefield Galleries, Sam smiled at Astrid, who pointed him toward Karena's office.

He was just about to knock when Paul Lakefield stepped up behind him.

"I thought your office had this under control, Mr. Desdune," he said in his heavy voice.

Sam turned, trying like hell not to let the things Karena had shared with him about her father pepper his dealings with the man. As he'd told Karena, he found it hard to believe that a man like Paul Lakefield didn't love his daughters. It just appeared he wanted to keep the women in his life in a certain place. That wasn't an entirely bad thing, just a pitifully stupid one.

"It's nice to see you again, Mr. Lakefield. As I assured you before, my firm is on top of the investigation."

"Then why didn't we know before now that the painting my daughter purchased belonged to the prince of Pirata?"

"Because for whatever reason the prince didn't want his ownership to be known until now."

"That's preposterous. Why would it be a secret?"

"I don't know, sir. That's what I intend to find out now."

"I don't want our name dragged through the mud over this. So you need to do whatever you can to keep that from happening."

"D&D Investigations is not into public relations, Mr. Lakefield. We'll find who sold the stolen painting to Karena and we'll find out the reason behind the secrecy in ownership. The rest, however, is up to you. Although, I might as well tell you that I don't think there's going to be any negative publicity on your end."

"How can you be so sure?"

"Because if they wanted to, the prince and princess could have already gone to the press with the fact that your gallery had purchased their stolen painting. It's been my experience that people don't take kindly to the theft of their property. The mere fact that we couldn't uncover the true ownership of the painting right off the bat tells me that there is more going on here than we know. More that has to do with the prince and princess protecting themselves or someone they know. And if that's the case, then they won't want this leaking to the press any more than you do."

Paul simply stared at him, as if trying to register the words Sam said. More like trying to judge the man who was speaking them to him. He didn't know how to take Sam, probably because Sam hadn't cowered to the older man's intimidating glares or authoritative tone from the beginning. In a lot of ways, Paul Lakefield reminded Sam of his own father. He was proud and distinguished and wanted what every man wanted for his family. Unfortunately, Sam thought, Lakefield was going about achieving that goal the wrong way. But this was neither the time nor the place to tell him that.

"You aren't quite what I expected," Paul admitted to Sam finally.

Sam tried not to shrug. "I'm not sure if that's a compliment or an insult."

Paul simply nodded. "It's definitely not an insult, son. As for the compliment, well, that remains to be seen. Shall we?" he said, reaching for the doorknob leading to Karena's office.

Sam inhaled and followed behind him. This was the man who was breaking Karena's heart, the man who by his actions was standing in the way of Sam's future with her. But for some odd reason, Sam couldn't find it in himself to dislike him. Go figure.

Chapter 17

If anybody ever asked, Karena would deny it until the day she died. But to herself, she had no choice but to admit seeing Sam walk through the door ahead of her father sent waves of relief washing through her body.

For the past hour, she and Monica had been speaking with the de Carrieros of Pirata, royalty with heavy South American accents and easy smiles.

Izabel was a lovely woman, tall and thinly built. Her long, flowing jet-black hair fell in thick waves down her back, held away from her face with diamond-encrusted combs. Her olive-toned skin was a complementary backdrop to deep brown eyes, and her ready smile had put Karena instantly at ease.

Felipe, as he'd asked her and Monica to call him, was taller than his wife, towering well above six feet in Karena's estimation. He wore a dark-colored suit that only made his darker complexion more apparent. On the lapel of his jacket was a green-and-yellow swatch of material covered with a gold brooch that Karena assumed was his family's official insignia. His hair was thick and wavy like his wife's but a lot less shiny.

They both sat in chairs pulled closer together, looking regal and at home at the same time.

Monica had a chair pulled on the same side of the desk as Karena. When Sam and her father walked in, Karena stood. So did Prince Felipe.

"Sam Desdune from D&D Investigations," Sam said, his glance moving over Karena swiftly then leaving reluctantly as he extended his hand to the prince. "It's a pleasure to meet you, Your Highness."

The prince took Sam's hand in a hearty shake. "Please. You must call me Felipe. And this," he said, motioning for her to stand, "is my wife, Izabel."

"Princess," Sam said, taking her hand and bringing it his lips.

Izabel smiled and Karena's heart began to race. He was just as good with royalty as he was with her and her staff.

"I'm Paul Lakefield, owner of Lakefield Galleries," her father said and was about to say something else when, to Karena's surprise, her mother walked in.

Well, well, well, the gang's all here, she thought to herself and tried not to sigh with frustration. Must everybody be here to witness her mistake?

"And I'm Noreen Lakefield, Paul's wife."

The prince and princess exchanged pleasantries and handshakes with the Lakefields. Astrid was called to bring in more chairs, but the astute receptionist suggested they simply move the meeting down the hall to the conference room.

Karena readily agreed with that idea and led the small crowd down the hall. As she walked, Sam came to stand beside her.

"Don't look so worried. We're going to get to the bottom

of this," he said seriously, reaching for the door to the conference room before she could and holding it open while she entered.

His words were even more comforting than his presence, and she mentally chastised herself for thinking that way. She shouldn't depend on him, shouldn't need him to get through this.

Once they were all seated, Sam took the lead.

"I understand you're here about the painting," he began.

"Yes," Prince Felipe said, holding up a hand to stop Sam from continuing. "And let me just explain how this has all come about. I am afraid it is partially my fault."

Karena held her breath, dreading the upcoming words. Sam scooted closer to her, taking her hand in his as they both waited.

"About four years ago my wife and I made a discovery. Our young son, Cezar, had a talent for painting. We did not pay the talent enough attention." Felipe sighed, his dark eyes looking sad for a moment. "To be honest, we did not pay it any attention at all. It was a hobby of his. We did not mind it so much as long as he did his schoolwork and studied his legacy."

"We should have supported him more," Izabel said quietly.

Karena watched as the pretty woman clenched her hands in her lap. She did not look down, as Karena had expected a princess to do while in the company of her husband. A foolish notion, she knew, especially given the way she felt about her mother always taking the stance behind her father. But this was royalty and she knew the rules of their game were vastly different from Americans'.

Still, Izabel de Carriero looked around at the women, her eyes melancholy but intelligent and aware of the mistake she felt she'd made.

Felipe nodded, reached down and squeezed his wife's hand. Simultaneously, Sam squeezed hers.

"Cezar was very passionate about his painting. So much that he sold one to a lady in our village. That lady gave the painting to a relative who lived in the United States. Then the lady began to get requests for more paintings. Cezar painted more and gave them to the lady."

Karena was stunned but didn't feel like everything had quite clicked into place.

"He has been painting and selling the pictures for three years now."

"But the painting we purchased was signed by an artist named Leandro," Monica said, her elegantly arched brows drawing close together in consternation.

Izabel smiled. "Cezar's second name is Leandro. He signed his portraits with that name so we would not know what he was doing. So that everyone would not know the paintings came from a royal."

Karena sat back in her chair with a sigh. She was speechless.

"How old is Cezar?" Sam asked.

"He is fourteen this month," Felipe said with a small smile. "Last week he came to us to admit what he had been doing. Feeling like fools, Izabel and I asked to see his studio. It was when he was showing us that he found a painting missing."

Finally pulling herself together, Karena spoke. "I don't understand. If nobody knew that Cezar was Leandro, how did the appraiser's report mention the royals?"

"Cezar has only the best materials. The paints and canvases he uses are obtained only by persons of wealth in our village. Royals. In his signature, right in the center of the *a,* he also drops a dot of fourteen-karat gold then presses it with a small replica of our seal." Felipe patted the insignia covering his chest pocket. "If you look closely, it will match this."

Paul rubbed his head then stood. "On behalf of my daughter and the Lakefield Galleries, I offer you and your family my apologies. We will return your merchandise immediately."

"No," Izabel responded, immediately coming out of her seat. "You do not understand. Cezar is good. His paintings should be shared with the world. We want them to be shared."

"Yes." Felipe nodded. "We want you to keep them and show them in your gallery."

"Are you sure?" Karena asked, flabbergasted at the turn of events.

"Perfectly," Izabel answered with a smile.

"Then we will pay you," Paul said, hastily reaching into his breast pocket for his checkbook.

"No. No." Felipe shook his head. "We will not hear of it. I know who took the painting. I will settle the matter when I return."

"We'd like to find the thief, as well," Sam said.

"No. There is more you do not understand. I must deal with him myself."

At that, there was a knock at the door. All eyes turned in that direction as Alexander Bennett walked in.

Chapter 18

"Alex!" Felipe smiled as he embraced his nephew.

Alexander Bennett, with his deep-brown skin and inky black hair, hugged Felipe back. "Good to see you again, Felipe."

"What's going on?" Monica had moved to Karena's side. "And who is he?"

It was Sam who answered. "Alexander Bennett. He's the CEO of Bennett Industries. His mother is from Brazil."

Monica eyed Alex suspiciously. Remembering their first conversation regarding Alex and Monica possibly hooking up, Karena watched her sister's reaction to the man carefully.

"So what's this I hear about stolen paintings?" Alex said after he'd hugged and kissed Izabel and all other introductions were made.

"It is Cezar. He has been painting and selling the paintings. We did not know until last week."

"Little C?" Alex asked, apparently surprised. "Wow, I had

my secretary pull some photos off the Internet. This Leandro's paintings are really good. I mean, Little C really has talent. Why the big secret?"

"Probably because we did not support him when he told us he wanted to paint."

Alex shook his head. "It's hard for a father to hear his son doesn't have the same career goals that he does."

With that comment, Karena looked at her father. She did have the same career goals as him, she just wasn't a son.

"Well, I'm glad this misunderstanding has been settled," Noreen said, moving to stand beside Izabel. "Now you must let us show you our city. We can have lunch and get to know each other."

Izabel practically beamed. "That would be nice. Thank you."

"Yes, you can show them around, Noreen. I will stay here and deal with the remnants of this botched deal," Paul said.

For a minute Karena's heart sank. He was obviously talking about dealing with her. But then to her shock, Noreen touched Paul's arm.

"No, I think it'll be better if you join us, dear. Surely the prince would love to talk about your colorful history and business acquisitions."

"I have to work, Noreen," Paul said tightly.

"Work can wait," she responded sternly.

Both Karena and Monica looked at each other.

"It will be great fun," Felipe said finally.

And in the next instant, the foursome were headed out of the conference room.

"I guess you're mother's not as weak-minded as you think," Sam whispered in Karena's ear.

She was about to say something when Alex Bennett approached them.

"So you're the one who purchased a stolen painting from

my royal relatives?" he said, looking at her with a decidedly pensive glare.

Straightening her shoulders, she extended a hand. "Karena Lakefield. It's nice to meet you, Mr. Bennett. I wish it were under better circumstances."

His medium-size lips spread into a slow grin as he took her hand, shaking it lightly. "The pleasure is all mine. When Sam called this morning, I could tell this was an important case to him. A personal case."

Karena tried not to blush.

"Personal, huh?" Monica questioned.

His attention instantly taken from Karena, Alex said, "And who might you be?"

"I might be Monica Lakefield, manager of this gallery," she answered in the frostiest tone Karena had ever heard her use.

"Alex—"

"I know who you are," she cut him off then turned her attention back to Karena. "Did he say 'personal'?"

"Yes, I did say personal. But that's just my assumption," Alex jumped in, giving Monica a look to match her snippy tone.

Out of the corner of her eye Karena could see Sam covering his mouth to hide a chuckle.

"Please excuse my sister, Mr. Bennett. I appreciate your coming in today, although I'm not real sure of your involvement."

"Let me clear that up," Sam said, still trying not to grin. "When I found out it was the prince and princess in your office, I called Alex. I knew he had family in Brazil and was hoping for an inside track on what we were dealing with. I didn't anticipate the prince and princess being so forthcoming."

She nodded her understanding.

"I got hung up in traffic or I would have been here sooner."

"Then I guess it's a good thing your assistance wasn't really needed."

"Monica," Karena gasped.

Alex held up a hand. "No. Don't apologize for her again. She's not a child. She's responsible for her own actions. Let her apologize for being rude."

Monica lifted her chin. "Not rude, just honest. And not charmed by a name, a fake smile, a designer suit and shiny Rolex." She turned to Karena. "I'll be in my office. Come see me when you're done here. Nice job, Sam," she said with a frown in his direction before walking out of the conference room.

"Dayum," Alex said once she was gone. "Excuse my language, but can it get any colder in here?"

"I'm sorry," Karena said.

"No, I told you it's not your place to apologize."

"She's not really that bad." She defended Monica even though she wanted to strangle her for her behavior.

"She's not?" Sam arched a brow.

Karena shot him a warning glare. "No. She's not. This has been rough on all of us."

"Don't worry about it. I'm not that easily offended. But I've got to say the dude who rained on her parade did one hell of a job."

"What?"

Sam and Alex exchanged a look.

"It's classic," Alex began. "A woman scorned will blister—again excuse my language—the balls off the very next man who makes her remember she's a living, breathing female." He shrugged. "But it's okay. I'm a busy man. I came here as a favor to Sam and it was nice to see my relatives again and to learn that my little cousin is a talented artist. As for your sister, she can continue to hibernate. I'm not in the habit of working to warm women up to me."

"I see," Karena said slowly, not sure if she liked his candor or not.

"Thanks for coming down, Alex," Sam interjected. "Can't believe the great Leandro is a fourteen-year-old."

"Tell me about it. My secretary sent me an entire portfolio on him. No pics. Just stats of how well his work is doing in the States and overseas. Felipe and Izabel better keep a close eye on him and his business dealings from now on."

"Yeah, I think they're getting it together now. Still want to know who actually stole the painting though," Sam said thoughtfully.

"Well, I've got a full afternoon ahead of me, so I'm going to get back on the road. Let me know if I can help with anything else."

Sam and Alex shook hands. "Will do."

"Again, nice meeting you, Karena," Alex said, leaning forward and kissing Karena on the cheek.

"Likewise," she said with a smile. She'd been watching the ease with which Alex and Sam got along. Sam was just like that, a genuinely likable person who people seemed drawn to. Even her father didn't seem as standoffish with him today.

Thinking of her father had her mind reverting to her mother and the way she'd stood up to her father just moments ago. She wondered what was going on there.

Unfortunately, she had other pressing matters to deal with.

Chapter 19

"How about lunch?" Sam asked the moment they were alone.

"Ah, I don't think that's a good idea," she replied quickly, as if she had no intention of even considering his question. "I've got a ton of work on my desk."

He should have known she'd say that. "How about dinner?"

"Sorry, Sam. Not tonight."

Not the answer he wanted.

"You have to eat," he countered.

She was moving just for the sake of moving, possibly to keep from moving directly to him. Sam watched her as she went around the large conference-room table, pushing in one chair after the other as if this, too, were her job.

"I know what I have to do, Sam. Despite what you may think, I don't need you to dictate my every move."

"Is that what you think I'm doing?"

Her back had been facing him and she whirled around with her answer. "It's what I know you're doing. Have dinner, Karena. Don't worry, Karena. Come to my house in the country, Karena. Every time you see me, you're giving orders."

"I'm suggesting dinner and you're accusing me of something else. Are you sure it's me you're angry with?"

"I never said I was angry," she said, standing behind a chair. She probably could have pulled off the look of indignation but for the way her fingers were digging into the back of the chair.

She wore a pantsuit today, navy blue. The waist-length jacket molded to her arms while the slacks fit her lower body like a glove. A thin silver blouse broke the monotony of the dark color, adding a flash of something fierce in her eyes.

During the meeting she'd been nervous and anxious. He'd wanted nothing more than to console her and for a moment thought his touch, his presence had done just that. But right now he wasn't entirely sure.

"Headache?" he asked when he saw her squinting, her shoulders slumping slightly.

She sighed. "I'm just tired."

He nodded and took a couple of steps until he stood beside her. Reaching out a hand, he rubbed the nape of her neck. "Close your eyes," he whispered.

It took a moment but finally she acquiesced. His fingers moved slowly, methodically over the tightened muscles. Coming to stand fully behind her, he put both hands on her shoulders and began to knead.

Initially she jumped, but he made a shooshing sound in her ear and she tried to relax. Beneath her clothes, he felt the taut muscles giving slightly to his ministrations. She was wound so tight it was a wonder she could stand or even think straight.

His fingers feathered over her neck, his thumbs pressing

into the nape. She moaned and he pushed harder, letting her body's reaction guide him further. Her head lolled forward, and he rubbed with a little more pressure.

"I know you're going to fight my words, and that's not my intent," he began, talking slowly, his voice moving right along with the movements of his hands. "You need to take better care of yourself, Karena. None of this is worth your health, your sanity."

Her shoulders began to tighten and he bent his head forward, kissed her temple. "Relax, baby. Just relax and let me take care of you."

"I…can take care of…myself," she said.

"I know you can," he responded, his lips moving over her temple. "But I want to. Let me, please, Karena, just let me love you."

She jerked then, moving quickly so that she was out of his grasp and his hands were still in position as if her neck were just beneath him. Sam blinked, trying to regain the moment he feared had been lost. "Baby," he began.

She held up a hand. "No. I'm fine." She licked her lips and took another precautionary step backward. "Really. I, um, I just have some things to catch up on."

Running, again. Sam sighed. "Karena."

"We'll have dinner," she said quickly. Too quickly. "Just let me finish up some things in the office and I'll meet you for dinner. Where do you want to go?"

Her gaze held his, her body standing defensively about three feet away from him now. He wanted to grab her, to hold her to him until she was soft and yielding in his arms again. But he knew better. He knew Karena.

"Meet me at Lucien's," he said, wanting her once again on his turf.

She nodded. "Fine. I can be there probably around six."

"Six it is," he agreed, and because he did want to take care of her, because he did—even though this was the first time he'd admitted it to himself—love her, Sam backed away. He moved to the door, turning to her once more and saying, "Get something for lunch, even if it's just a sandwich. Put something in your stomach and take something for your headache before it gets too bad."

Again Karena nodded and watched as he left her alone in the conference room, while her insides swirled like a building storm.

Let me love you, that's what he'd said. Was it really what he'd meant?

"So anyway, when I went into her room, Mama was packing. I asked where she was going, and she just said away." Deena was talking in her quick, rushed tone.

Karena rubbed her temple as she held the phone to her ear. Two hours ago she'd taken aspirin; now she wondered if she'd taken enough.

"Away?"

"Yeah, that's what I said," Deena continued. "She said she and Daddy needed to talk, to work some things out."

"Work what things out?"

"I was wondering that myself, so you know I asked. She assured me it was nothing like divorce or anything. She just said it was a conversation long overdue. And I thought, wow, I wonder what this is all about. But then Daddy came in, you know all serious with that big vein in the middle of his forehead bulging. So I was like, well, when are you coming back? Daddy shrugged and said, 'Whenever your mother feels she's said her piece, I guess.'" The last had been said in Deena's husky imitation of Paul Lakefield.

"But I don't understand," Karena said.

"You know what, K? I don't think we're supposed to

understand. They're our parents after all, and it's common knowledge that kids don't understand their parents."

"We're not kids, Deena. We're grown women. It's not a stretch to know that something's going on between them."

"I know that, K. I wasn't saying it like we're too young to know or should be too young to care. All I'm saying is that whatever it is, it's between them. Clearly Mama has it under control, so I really don't think there's anything for us to worry about."

"If you didn't think we should worry, why'd you call me right away with the news?" Because really, Karena could have gone for the next twenty-four hours without any more major revelations.

"Because they're our parents and I felt you should know they'd be out of town. What's with this crabby attitude of yours? And where's Monica? I called her office but she wasn't there. And for the life of me I can't imagine where else the Ice Queen would be besides work."

Karena sighed. "Don't call her that. She's our sister."

"And that's why I'm allowed to call her that. Now, the minute somebody else calls her out of her name, it's on."

The smile crept across her lips, the chuckle erupting from her throat on impulse. Deena was impossible.

"So they left town. Did you manage to at least get their destination?"

"You know I did," she said with a smile.

Yeah, Karena did know. When Deena wanted to know something, there was nothing any of them could do to keep it from her. "Well?"

"Oh, they're going to the vacation house in Martha's Vineyard. But we're not to tell any of Daddy's business associates and we're not to disturb them unless one of us is bleeding from the head and knocking on death's door. Mama's orders."

Again Karena chuckled. "I know Mama did not say that."

"Nope, I added that part, but you know what I mean."

"Yeah, Dee, I know what you mean."

"So what's going on with you? You sound terrible."

"Gee, thanks," Karena answered glibly just as a knock sounded at her door. "Listen, I've gotta go. I'll call you later."

"How about breakfast tomorrow? I've got news to share," Deena offered.

"Sure, since you're home alone, I'll come by the house."

"Sounds good, but bring food. I'm not cooking and I'm not keeping that silly housekeeper in the house when Daddy's not here."

"I feel you on that one," Karena said, never understanding why her father hired a housekeeper when her mother still did all the cooking and cleaning herself. "So I'll see you around ten."

"Cool. Be safe."

"You, too." Karen disconnected the phone, saying, "Come in," simultaneously.

She hadn't expected who walked in.

"I'm sorry to disturb you. This morning you looked as if you were still perplexed, and I had some free time while Felipe took care of some international business at the embassy. So I figured I would come by and talk with you."

Izabel de Carriero stood in her doorway, looking as if she really thought she was intruding. Karena hurried from her chair around the desk. "Oh, please, don't apologize," she said, motioning for Izabel to take a seat and closing the door behind her. "You're quite welcome here."

"Thank you," Izabel responded as she sat.

Going back around her desk, Karena took her seat. "So the grand tour of Manhattan is over?"

"Yes. Your parents are delightful people."

"Ah, my mother loves to play hostess. My father, on the other hand…"

"Actually, your mother was most vocal and wanted to know just as much about my home as I did hers. A very intelligent woman, I think she is. Your father is very formidable, as well."

Formidable seemed to be an understatement but at least, Karena thought, he'd been civil to her.

"I'm glad to hear that, Izabel."

"Yet, you are still worried?"

"No."

"You are. I see the lines of worry on your face."

Karena wished a hole would miraculously appear and she'd be gulped into the dismal abyss of embarrassment. She really had to do something about these frown lines. "I'm fine." She heard herself saying this and grimaced inwardly as it sounded like a recording.

"You want to know who stole Cezar's paintings and sold them to you."

She could have continued to deny anything was wrong, could have called on her business training and familial etiquette. But she sensed the princess would see right through the charade. "Yes," she answered honestly.

Izabel nodded. "His name is Eduardo Matos. He is the brother of the woman, Iracema, who first sold Cezar's work."

Karena was appalled. "Why? How?"

"You must first understand that Pirata is a small town. We are granted self-administration by the República Federativa do Brasil. This means that we abide by the federal constitution but our local law is separate. And just like in your country, there are the rich and there are the poor."

"And Eduardo is poor?"

"He is not royalty. His family, however, lives in one of the larger villas near the shore. His mother used to work for the battalion chief who lived there. When he died he left the villa to her. She raised her two children there until her death several years ago. Eduardo and Iracema live there together. He is good with his hands, so he takes odd jobs in the village to help make enough money to keep the villa intact. Iracema sews well and makes her living this way."

"So they stole Cezar's paintings to make money to take care of their home?" Karena didn't understand. In her mind, stealing was a crime, no matter what the reason. And it was one of the worst crimes, right up there in her book with lying, because she felt they were both so damned unnecessary.

"No," Izabel shook her head. "There is an orphanage in Pirata, one of only a few Christian missions left in all of Brazil. This is where some of what are called the *meninos de rua* or 'street children' live."

"Street children?" It sounded like a term from a movie, not what children would be called in real life.

"Yes. These are abandoned or runaway children whom radicals in my country have targeted. About sixteen years ago eight street children were gunned down as they slept near the Candelària Church in downtown Rio de Janeiro. This brought more attention to the problems of the street children, as they faced elimination. Eduardo began taking in the street children he saw in Pirata, to keep them safe.

"It is unfortunate that Felipe and I are just now finding out about the shelter that Eduardo is providing, as he is proud and would not ask for help, especially from political figures such as the prince and I. Forgive me if I make my husband and myself seem as if we are out of touch with our village. It is that so much, what do you call it, red tape, is involved with being a royal."

Karena nodded, feeling as if she understood what the woman was trying to say.

"Well, we are going to fix that. But Eduardo, he has been like the caretaker at the orphanage. He and Elisabete Alvares. They are trying to take care of at least fifty street children of different ages. It is hard, because they do not have the funds needed. Eduardo sold you the painting to get money for the orphanage."

Karena had felt those words coming. Still they pricked her heart and she sat silently for the next few seconds.

"We paid half a million dollars for one painting," she finally said softly.

"In Pirata, that is enough to rebuild their building. Construction has already started, but there is still much to be done. So you see now why Felipe and I came here. We wanted to explain about Cezar and his work, but we also wish for you to let us handle Eduardo."

"I see. Certainly." Karena swallowed, took a deep breath. "I'll tell Sam to stop looking for him. It ends here," she said with finality.

"Obrigado," Izabel said with a smile. "Thank you."

"You're welcome," Karena responded.

"Would you like to see it?"

"See what?"

"The orphanage. I talked with your mother about it and she had many questions. She and your father have gone for a *ferias,* but if you are not too busy you can come to Pirata to see."

"Me? Come to Pirata?" It wasn't as if she'd never been there. She had been, right at the villa of Eduardo and Iracema Matos, she believed. But did she want to go back? Did she really want to see the man who had brought all this drama to her life? Even if he had good reason?

The answer was simple.

"Yes. I'd love to come to Pirata."

Chapter 20

It had taken only twenty minutes of waiting in the Harlem location of Lucien's before Sam realized she wasn't coming.

That and the phone call he received as he was walking out of the restaurant.

"Desdune."

"Hey, just wanted to check in with you before I left for the night."

It was Bree.

"Go ahead."

"Alex said you okayed me assigning an undercover to provide extra security for the prince and princess, so I sent that guy we have in New York already. Anyway, he just called to say the royal jet is being fueled up, estimated time of departure is three and a half hours."

"I guess they're in a hurry to get back home," Sam was saying as he crossed the street to his car, pressing the remote to unlock the doors.

It was when he was settled behind the steering wheel that Bree decided to drop her bombshell.

"There's another passenger listed on the manifest. An American. Her passport's already been scanned."

Sam's jaw twitched as he sat back against his leather seats. "Go on."

"It's Karena."

He cursed. Loudly. Fluently.

On the other end, Bree clucked her teeth. "Precisely the reaction I assumed you'd have. That's why I called right away."

"What the hell is she doing?"

"Come on, Sam, I'm sure you know."

Squeezing the bridge of his nose, he tried to take slow, even breaths. Otherwise, he was liable to punch something or someone. "Bree, I don't have time for this."

"You don't have time to listen to me warn you about scaring her away?"

"What? You don't have any idea what you're talking about. I'm not what's scaring her."

"You sure about that, big brother? You weren't the smartest guy when it came to your last relationship."

"Please, don't even compare Karena to Leeza." There was no comparison there. Leeza was a controlling, manipulative socialite with a split personality who had Sam walking on eggshells one minute and singing her praises the next. Ending things with her remained the best decision he'd ever made. No, Karena was nothing like that. And what he felt for Karena was nothing like what he'd imagined he felt for Leeza.

"I'm not comparing them. I'm comparing you. The man you were with Leeza and the one you are to Karena. It's one and the same."

"Bree, I've got to go."

"Just listen to me for a minute, Sam. A fool could see you've got feelings for her, but you need to make sure those feelings are reciprocated before you go pushing your way into her life. Don't forget I'm the one who knows you just about as well as you know yourself. You may think Karena Lakefield is the woman for you, the one you want to love, marry and cherish forever. But she may have another idea entirely." Bree sighed. "Just food for thought."

He couldn't be angry with her. She was just being Bree. She was being his sister, his twin, one of his closest friends. "Thanks," he said solemnly then started his car's engine.

"Don't look for me in the office tomorrow."

On the other end Bree smiled. She knew exactly what he was saying. "I'll let Mom and Dad know you're out of the country."

With a grim smile of his own, Sam thanked her again and disconnected. His foot lay heavily on the gas as he needed to make his way back to his house, pack and get to the private airstrip where the de Carrieros' jet was parked.

Using speakerphone so he could concentrate on driving, he called Alex and asked him to contact the de Carrieros and get clearance for him to travel with them. Once that was done, he let his mind return to the pressing matter at hand.

Karena.

The look he gave her was one of barely restrained anger. His usually calm brown eyes were simmering, his lips tight in consternation as he boarded the jet just moments before it was to take off.

In that instant Karena remembered their dinner plans, her reluctance to go and finally the moment Izabel offered for her to fly back to Brazil with her.

No wonder he was angry. She'd stood him up.

Izabel and Felipe were already buckled into their seats toward the front of the jet, leaving Karena seated in the middle section of seats, behind a small table and minibar. Her heart hammered as she turned away from him. At that exact moment Sam looked away from her as well, both their gazes locking on the seat next to her.

He was going to sit there, even though there were two more seats behind her. She knew with absolute certainty he was going to stop right beside her.

"Surprised to see me?" he asked the moment he was seated and had clicked the seat belt around his waist.

"A little," she replied honestly.

"I must have really wanted to have dinner with you to pack my bags and hop on a plane to Brazil."

His tone was clipped. He was really upset with her.

"Look, Sam, I'm sorry. I totally forgot. Izabel came to my office and we talked. She told me who stole the paintings and why and then offered to take me to meet him. I couldn't pass up the offer."

"And you couldn't call me to say that ahead of time? You had to just jump at the opportunity to leave me sitting at that restaurant waiting for you."

"It wasn't like that."

"Then what was it like? You set the time, Karena. I waited for you."

She took a deep breath, realizing that nothing she said was an acceptable excuse. She was wrong and when that was the case, Karena had no problem admitting it.

"I apologize. I should have called you."

He looked away from her then said simply, "Tell me about this thief."

And just like that, the comfort zone she always morphed to when they were together cloaked her. Her heart slowed to a normal beat as the jet took off and she settled in to tell Sam the story of Eduardo and the orphanage.

Chapter 21

The city of Pirata was located just east of Fortaleza, Brazil. It was a chic beachside town that very much resembled a scaled-down Miami to Karena.

The de Carrieros' villa was like an oasis. Tall, swaying palm trees, grass that looked as if millions of tiny emeralds had been tossed onto the ground, and a large crystalline-blue pond anchored the land the main house occupied. The main house was bright and cheerful, painted a delightful shade of coral and accented with beautiful dark brickwork. White doors, windows and railings gave it a tropical air, while the surrounding acres of property resonated royalty.

Around the main house were smaller homes, similar to the one she stayed at when she'd met with Eduardo.

It hadn't escaped her that the villa she'd visited him at was probably only miles away from this one. She remembered the Pirata Cathedral and the handicraft markets as they'd driven into town from the airport just a few short weeks ago.

Beside her in the Hummer, Sam sat perfectly still. He was wearing cream-colored linen slacks and matching shirt and was ten times as sexy as Phillip Michael Thomas as Tubbs in *Miami Vice*.

On the flight over she'd told him all about Eduardo and the orphanage, to which he'd been just as surprised as she was. When she thought he'd still want to recover the money she'd paid Eduardo, he'd immediately understood her need to see the orphanage personally. It wasn't actually said, but they both knew she wouldn't ask for the money back and there would be no prosecution of Eduardo.

His easy understanding was just one more tally in the pro column for Sam Desdune—a fact she wasn't entirely pleased with. Exactly when this thing between them had become more than lust, Karena wasn't sure. What she was sure of was the guidelines she'd given for their involvement. Of course, they hadn't spoken about it on the flight, but she knew the subject would arise. It was, after all, why he'd followed her here. But this time, Karena was determined to make Sam understand.

After sharing a late lunch on the blue-and-white-tiled balcony just off the main dinning room, Izabel, Sam and Karena had once again piled into the Hummer for their trek to the orphanage.

Karena kept her gaze out the window as they drove through the small town of Pirata. She was again looking for the villa where she had first met Eduardo, but instead the Hummer came to a stop near what looked like a warehouse, about the length of three row houses put together.

The building was a sickly green color, chipping paint from the bottom that rested on browning grass to the roof that looked as if it would collapse at any moment. The rusted door at the front opened and out ran two boys, maybe between the ages of ten and fifteen. They were thin, their clothes clean but too small. Surrounding the house was a wooden gate that was missing more than a few planks.

It took a second before Karena realized Sam was calling her name, waiting for her to exit the vehicle. When she did, he extended his hand to her and she readily took it, returning her gaze to the two children who now walked to the edge of the gate.

"Olà! Està Eduardo aqui?" Izabel said, reaching over the gate to rub the head of the shortest boy.

He must have immediately recognized the insignia on the Hummer and then again on the small brooch Izabel wore on the sheer scarf at her neck, because he instantly bowed in a curtsy so deep Karena thought his head would touch the ground.

"No. Por favor. Isso não é necessário. De pé," she said in a soft voice.

Beside Karena, Sam bent to whisper in her ear. "She's telling him it's not necessary to bow to her and she's asking to see Eduardo."

Stunned, she looked up at him. "You speak Portuguese?"

Sam nodded. "I have this thing about foreign languages. Bree says its weird, but I speak about eight different languages."

Karena never would have guessed. While she knew a little Portuguese, enough to get her from the airport to the villa where she'd met Eduardo to be exact, she was in no way fluent in the language. In her travels for the gallery, she'd picked up bits and pieces of different languages as well as customs of different countries, but she'd never had the time to truly dedicate herself to completely learning a language.

The two boys were stepping aside, letting Izabel, who looked back to beckon Sam and Karena, into the building. Once inside, Karena sucked in a breath.

"There is much work that needs to be done," Izabel said

immediately. "Very little money is allotted to urban areas here. That is something that Felipe and I are working to change."

"Sounds just like the United States," Karena said.

"Yeah, even in our major cities, urban areas are suffering while the rich keep getting richer," Sam added.

"We want to work with Eduardo to make the living better for the children."

Moving through a long hall, Karena peeked into several open doors. One room was clearly a bedroom where twin-size cots were lined along the walls. In the center were two six-foot tables that held books with yellowed and tattered pages.

Another room held more tables, but these had benches. Probably the cafeteria. The next room held smaller tables and smaller chairs and a chalkboard. There were toys scattered about the floor, old, broken and overused toys.

Then out of one of the closed doors came a man. The same man Karena had met with weeks ago. Eduardo.

Their eyes met, and for a minute she thought he would run. Instead he squared his shoulders, bowing slightly at Izabel's approach.

"Princess, you have returned."

Izabel smiled as Eduardo reached for her hand and kissed its back. "I promised I would," she said in a regal tone. "This time I have brought Ms. Lakefield and Mr. Desdune to see your facility."

Eduardo released Izabel's hand and nodded toward Sam and Karena.

"Why didn't you just tell me about the children?" Karena asked instantly.

"Would you have given me half a million dollars to take care of them?" he asked with barely masked hostility. "You are rich, and rich people do not help poor people. Not if they know that is what they are doing."

His words took Karena aback and she flinched slightly. Sam was there, wrapping an arm around her waist.

"That's an unfair assumption, don't you think?" Sam asked. "Maybe if you'd tried being honest you would get more help."

Eduardo gave a dry chuckle. "It does not work that way here, sir."

Sam didn't respond because he knew it didn't work that way all over the world. Brazil was not alone in its treatment of the more unfortunate.

Late afternoon turned into evening as Eduardo led them through the facility, giving brief histories of some of the children as well as what he planned to do with the new funds he'd received from Karena. His partner, Elisabete, whom Karena suspected was also his girlfriend, was away picking up two unwanted babies from a family in Rio de Janeiro. Eduardo explained that they had been getting lots of calls from parents without money to care for their children, who did not want them to fall into the streets. Eduardo readily took them in, although he scarcely had the money to take care of them himself.

The entire setup had left Karena feeling melancholy and completely exhausted.

It had also given her an idea. One she'd have to wait until she got back to the States to implement.

Chapter 22

Karena felt like an idiot.

Not just because the real Leandro had turned out to be a child, but because she'd spent the past couple of weeks wanting desperately to hate this person for his duplicity, to make him pay for the drama he'd caused in her life. And now, after all was said and done, all she could do was feel sympathy for the circumstances that led Eduardo to do what he'd felt necessary.

It had been hours since her visit to the orphanage. She and Sam had shared a late meal in the kitchen of Izabel's house and she'd hurried off to bed, desperately needing some time to herself. As she lay in the bed, her mind had quickly reverted to the dozen or so children she'd seen in desperate need of everything, from food to shoes, to even clean blankets to cover them in the chilly nights. Her heart wept for them as well as for the man who tried to run the orphanage, the man who struggled without money from the government or anyone else to help him take care of these forgotten children.

Unable to sleep, she now walked along the beach that stretched around the property belonging to the prince and princess. In a few days she'd be on her way back to the city. On her way back to the life she'd become so accustomed to, the life that seemed so petty and insignificant, so materialistic and inconsequential compared with the plight of the children at the orphanage.

It was beautiful here, with the palace in the backdrop, the high ivy-covered walls guarding it like a fortress. And just below those walls the dense foliage with the almost-hidden path that she'd walked down barefoot—her sandals dangling from her fingers—until the warm sand tickled between her toes. She was just close enough that when the tide came in, it brushed against her ankles in a cool sprinkle of warm water.

She walked what seemed like aimless steps as thoughts whirled throughout her mind. And then, with the scenery was so perfect that the mood was set almost as if it had been scripted, she heard his voice calling her name.

"Karena."

She didn't turn but stopped walking, waiting for the inevitable touch.

The moment his hands rested on her shoulders, Karena melted against him. It felt so right, was so easy, to let him hold her. Moving his hands down her bare arms, he embraced her.

"What are you doing out here in the middle of the night?" he whispered against her ear because the sound of the rushing waves was louder down here on the beach than it had been from the balcony of her room.

"I need to think."

"I know what you mean. Eduardo gave us a lot to think

about. Sometimes you can get so caught up in your own life, your own problems, that you forget that somebody else might be doing a lot worse than you."

"I want to help him."

"I figured as much. What are you going to do? Refer him to the Lakefield Foundation?"

"I was thinking of referring him to my mother," she said, for the first time voicing the thoughts she'd been having for hours.

Sam was quiet for a minute, and she was almost sure he was thinking of a way to put the words he wanted to say.

"Don't set yourself up for disappointment," he finally managed.

Karena sighed. "I just want so much more for her."

"She has to want more for herself, baby. You can't give her a life that's not right for her."

"I know," Karena reluctantly admitted. "I'm going to suggest it and let her take it from there."

"Good girl," he said, and she could hear he was smiling.

"You say that as if I've done something to please you."

He was holding her tighter and Karena loved the feeling. His breath whispered over the sensitive skin of her neck each time he spoke, and she could feel her nipples tightening.

"You always please me, Karena. Except when you're being hardheaded."

At that she gave a little chuckle. "Let's not talk about the latter right now," she said, slowly turning in his embrace. "I'd rather hear more about how I can please you."

It was risky, she knew, but she wanted him. No, tonight she *needed* him.

"I'm a simple man, remember, who likes simple things." His voice had turned deeper, his fingers running through her short hair until his hands were cupping the back of her head.

Around them a warm breeze blew, the evening tide washed up against the shore, crashing loudly against the sand. The spot where they were standing was pretty secluded, not to mention dark since it was well after midnight. But none of that mattered.

Karena let her eyes flutter shut as Sam's lips touched her forehead. The thin material of the cover-up she'd slipped over her night shorts and sports bra clung to her skin as her body heated.

Dropping featherlight kisses all over her face, Sam whispered her name repeatedly, until her mind was completely full of him.

Bringing her palms to his chest, Karena leaned forward, kissing his hard pectoral muscles through the white undershirt he wore tucked into dark basketball shorts. He sucked in a breath as she moved over slightly, taking his small nipple into her mouth. His hand tightened at the back of her neck and Karena's heart thumped with desire.

To say she wanted him, needed him, was definitely an understatement. They were miles and miles away from home, away from her family and the pressure she felt she was under. They were on a beautiful beach in South America, just the two of them. She felt like the famous saying, "What happens in Vegas, stays in Vegas." Only they weren't in Vegas, there were no bright lights and cha-chinging slot machines.

There was only her and Sam.

Slipping her hands down his sides, she lifted the shirt up and over his head then flattened her tongue over the ridges of his chest once more. He stood perfectly still, letting her have her way. The power of lust ripped through her with ferocity similar to the waves of water just a few feet away.

Emboldened by that power, Karena kissed lower until her tongue slipped into the indentation of his navel.

"Baby," he whispered, his voice dying slowly as she used both hands to slide his shorts down his muscled legs.

The salty seawater scent of the Atlantic Ocean wafted through the air as Karena's lips grazed his lower stomach. Her small hands had returned to his hips, moved around to cup his taut buttocks. Again his hands were cupping her head, holding her still.

"I'm a simple man, baby," he said hoarsely.

She looked up at him, saw the mere slits his eyes had become, the ragged in-and-out movement of his chest, the tiny muscle ticking in his jaw.

"And I simply want to please you," she whispered, licking her lips only seconds before lowering her head to lick the tip of his aroused penis.

His fingers flexed, released her head then rested on her shoulders. She shifted again, anchoring her knees in the sand, keeping one hand on his buttocks but moving the other to wrap around the base of his length. Using only perception to guide her, she lowered her head once more, positioning her mouth over him before using her tongue to lick the underside.

The muscles in his buttocks clenched as he moaned. She opened her mouth wider, took him in slowly, all the while using her tongue to massage his pulsating member.

It was intoxicating, this power mixed with the musky, all-male taste of him. It was more than she'd ever experienced in her life. Emotions swirled through her in a tidal wave as she continuously worked her lips over him. He was gasping for breath, digging his fingers into her shoulders as he stood at her mercy.

She didn't just want him or need him. It was deeper than that, and at this very moment she knew it, felt it and let the fear mix with the interminable pleasure inside.

When he pulled away from her and pushed her back onto the sand, Karena was breathless. Bending over her, it took him less than five seconds to rip the cover-up away and pull her shorts down. The moment the material was free from her ankles, he was lifting her legs, anchoring them on each of his shoulders and driving his penis, still damp from her ministrations, into her center.

She gasped at the force of entry, digging her nails into his biceps. His hips moved with quick, deathly precision as he thrust deeply inside of her before pulling almost all the way out and repeating the action again.

He was filling her, taking her in measured steps, but with enough force that she knew it was serious. This wasn't just sex, it had surpassed that level long ago. Tears stung the backs of her eyes, even as she reached up, wrapped her arms around his neck to pull him closer.

It seemed like forever that he thrust inside of her, then suddenly not long enough when her body shivered, her release covering him only moments before he joined her.

Seconds ticked by as they lay on the beach, sand rubbing against her back while the weight of Sam's body cocooned her front.

She was quiet, her heart just settling to a normal rhythm when he lifted a bit, cupped her face in his hands and said in the words of such a simple man, "I love you, Karena."

Chapter 23

He hadn't said the words once in the next two days they were in Pirata.

Did she want him to?

Hell no! That's why she kept moving through their outings and lovemaking as if nothing were missing. Because nothing was.

The words weren't needed. Weren't wanted.

Besides, they were like a broken record with the needle permanently stuck repeating them over and over again in her mind. If Sam had actually said them again, she probably would have screamed.

Yet Karena would be a fool not to admit that the time spent with Sam was more than wonderful, more than anything she'd ever expected with a man. But Sam was perfect. She already knew and accepted that.

So why was she sitting on the plane beside him wondering

how to approach the subject of their relationship—the rules of their relationship?

In a little under an hour they'd be landing on a private airstrip just north of LaGuardia. He would probably want to share a car to her apartment then head on to his house in Connecticut.

The house she'd dreamed about last night.

It was silly, she knew, and she whispered the same to herself as she'd crept out of the bed she and Sam were sharing to go into the bathroom and splash water onto her face. It was just a house, a building built on a wonderful piece of land. It wasn't the answer to all her hopes and dreams, the ones she kept tucked deep in the recesses of her mind. It wasn't her salvation.

To top all that off, it wasn't hers. She owned her condo overlooking Central Park. She loved the walks she took through the park and sometimes even farther to work. The city was refreshing and energizing, it was where she wanted, no, needed to be. Why? Because it was her choice.

"What are you over there thinking so hard about?"

She actually jumped at the sound of his voice, feeling as if he'd been eavesdropping on her private thoughts. Giving herself a shake for silliness, she mustered a smile and looked over at him. "Nothing."

His brows raised and she sighed. He always knew. Well, no time like the present.

She cleared her throat. "Okay, I was thinking about us."

At that he smiled and reached for her hand, entwining their fingers as if they were juveniles walking down the street. "Good thoughts, I hope."

She nodded. "Yes. I think they're good." He lifted her hand, kissed the back of it and continued to smile at her. Oh, boy, this was a little harder than she'd anticipated.

"So, were you thinking of all the wonderfully sinful things you'd like to do to my body when we get home?"

He sucked one fingertip into his mouth and she felt a shiver of warmth etch down her spine. "Ah, no, not exactly."

"Hmm, then maybe you're thinking of all the wonderfully sinful things you want me to do to your body when we get home?"

Home. Why did he keep saying that?

"I was thinking that we could maybe see each other for dinner once during the week and then rotate spending weekends together," she said in a rushed voice before his touch made her forget everything but her name.

Sam paused instantly, the finger that was in his mouth slipping out slowly. His hand placed hers gently on the arm of the seat as he sat back eyeing her closely.

"Are those your terms?" he asked solemnly.

"I wouldn't make it sound as serious as 'terms.' I just thought it would be good to set aside enough time so we could be together. Isn't that what you want?"

He was nodding, but Karena had the sinking suspicion he wasn't agreeing with her.

"So what's this, like, the negotiation stage? You suggest a schedule, then I suggest one and we meet somewhere in the middle? Sort of a relationship mediation."

"I'm not liking your sarcasm, Sam."

"Good, because I'm not liking your idiotic suggestion."

"Don't call me names!"

"Don't change the subject. You know damned well I'm not calling you names. I'm telling you that what you're suggesting is crazy. When two people decide to pursue a relationship they just do it, they don't pencil each other in the BlackBerry. That's not how it works."

"Well, Mr. Relationship Master, tell me how it does work.

Or better yet, tell me again why it didn't work between you and Leeza."

He looked incredulous. "What? Why are you even bringing her up? I told you about Leeza when we were in Maryland two months ago."

"Yes. You did. You told me how you met her, thought she was the one, proposed and then had a change of heart because she wanted to manipulate you, change you into the man she wanted you to be."

"And how does this relate to us?"

"What do you want from 'us,' Sam? What do you foresee happening with us?"

He dragged a hand down his face as if he were growing tired of this conversation. Well, she didn't care. They were going to get this over with. She had limitations, whether Sam Desdune liked them or not, and he could either deal with them or he couldn't. Better she find out now before her own feelings grew too out of control.

"I love you, Karena. Love to me means forever. So having dinner with you once a week and alternate weekends just isn't enough. I want to see you every day, hear your voice when I close my eyes at night to go to sleep, see your face when I wake each morning to face the day. I want it all."

And although her heart hammered in her chest and her head throbbed as if someone was using it for a bongo, this was exactly what she was afraid of.

"I want you to move in with me. I think the house away from the city would be good for you, good for your stress level. I want to take care of you, to love you."

"When did you ask me what I wanted?"

"Excuse me?"

"When…did…you stop planning your little fairy tale to find out what I wanted? Because I would think that should matter, since I'd be the one uprooting and changing my entire life. I'd be the one bending to your will."

Why did she do this? Why was she twisting everything he said to make it seem wrong?

"I thought we had a great time together these past few days."

"We did," she said, sighing. "And we did when I was at your place. Look, Sam, I know there's something between us. I accept that and I'm willing to take the chance to see where it goes. But I can't just jump blindly, giving you everything without considering what's best for me."

"You don't think having a place to come home to after leaving the gallery, a place that will let you completely relax—you don't think that's best for you?"

"I can relax at my place."

"But you don't. You work and you take your sister's calls and you work some more. You don't relax and you don't make time for yourself."

"So now the suggestion is to move to your place *and* cut off my family? You're out of your mind. I'd never ask that of you."

"And I'm not asking it of you. I'm telling you that you need to learn to live for you, to make decisions that will be best for you."

"That's what I'm doing."

He knew it had been coming, it always did. Sam Desdune had a breaking point. He had a line that once was crossed, there was no coming back from. Karena had just stepped one foot over it.

There was the telltale drop, slight shake of the plane and then definite touchdown of the wheels hitting asphalt. They'd landed. And they'd ended.

"I won't lie to you, Karena. This is not how I work. I'm a

marriage-and-family kind of guy. I thought we were on the same wavelength there. I guess I was wrong."

"You know how I feel about marriage, about giving up everything that I am for a man."

"Not a man, Karena. Your man. Your husband. And it's not about giving up everything that you are, but about entering into a relationship that will make you both as one. I would never ask you to give up who you are for me. But I won't sacrifice what I need, either."

She'd been in the process of unsnapping her seat belt when her head shot up and she glared at him. "What are you saying?"

"I'm saying that you have a choice, you can step out of that box you've created for yourself using your mother and her decisions as a crutch, or you can act like the independent, sophisticated woman I fell in love with and take a chance on me, on love, on yourself." Then he shrugged. "It's that simple."

Karena stood slowly, being careful to take deep breaths, hoping to calm the fierce anger growing inside her. "Is that an ultimatum?"

Sam stood, walked to her and let his finger trace the line of her jaw. "It's my final offer."

Chapter 24

A week later Karena sat in her office going through her mail. Halloween was last week, and she'd spent the evening alone in her condo with art catalogs spread out around her, a cup of flat soda since she'd let the ice cubes melt in it and a headache that just would not quit.

Today she felt a little better, just a little. She was moving robotically but refused to believe it had anything to do with the last words she and Sam had shared. She hadn't spoken to him since they'd both climbed out of the jet. He'd let her get into the waiting car and called himself a taxi. She wanted desperately to argue how stupid that was and that they could share, but she really didn't think that was possible.

How dare he give her an ultimatum and then expect her to answer at the raise of his eyebrows. He'd taken the word *arrogant* to another level, one on which she was not about to go with him.

If that's how he was used to dealing with women, then she

didn't need to be in that group. The decision to let him in even marginally was hard enough to make. She knew it would be a big mistake to give in to his ultimatum and give him the impression that he'd always win that way with her.

Hell no, that just wasn't the life she predicted for herself. Still, it had her wondering what exactly her future held.

With a sigh, she opened the next envelope and read the ecru-and-brown-embossed invitation with a feeling of warmth spreading through her.

In the spirit of peace and joy
this holiday season
Mr. and Mrs. Reginald St. Claire
request the honor of your presence
at the marriage of their daughter
Tia Marisal
to
Trenton Desmond Donovan
on the twenty-fourth of December
at six o'clock in the afternoon
Mt. Charleston Resort
Las Vegas, Nevada

They were getting married. Another couple was making the ultimate commitment to each other. All she could do for the next few minutes was stare at the invitation. Inside the envelope amongst the thin slip of paper and a card with all the information pertaining to the resort and making reservations, was a response card.

At first she'd thought it a no-brainer. Of course she would go. The Donovans had come to be like extended family to her through Noelle. In fact, they were Noelle's family, and since

Noelle was her best friend, she should have been rushing to fill out the card and put it back in the mail. But she wasn't.

"Girl, I swear I think you were born with that serious look on your face," Noreen said as she made her way into Karena's office.

"Mama," Karena said, looking up quickly because she hadn't heard anyone knock on the door, nor had she heard her mother enter, but she was already taking a seat.

"Whatever it is, Karena, believe me it can't be that bad."

Hurriedly she started putting the invitation and its accompaniments into the envelope. "It's nothing," Karena replied.

"I hope you're going to respond to that before you tuck it away into your drawer," Noreen said, looking down at Karena's desk.

"Ah, yeah. I just need to check my calendar first and then I'll send my response in."

Noreen nodded. "Good, because it's rude to ignore an invitation. RSVPs are sent for a reason. And it's not hard to simply reply. Some folk are just so tacky."

With the invitation pushed to the side of her desk, Karena sat up in her chair. "So how was the getaway?"

Noreen smiled. And it was different from before. Karena was intrigued.

"The getaway was fantastic. Your father and I really made some progress."

"Really?"

"Yes, and that's why I'm here. I want to talk to you about your trip to Pirata."

"Oh. That was really nice, too. I had the chance to meet Eduardo Matos. He's the guy who sold me the painting."

"Izabel told me all about him. And I'm telling you, Karena, my heart just ached for those children. I knew right then what must be done."

"I had some thoughts about helping the children, as well."

Noreen held up a hand to stop her from talking. "Let me just get this out before I lose my nerve."

Karena's lips clapped shut and she sat back in her chair, waiting.

"Remember we talked about the foundation and me wanting to get involved? Well, the moment Izabel told me about Eduardo and those children I knew I'd found my cause. I want to help them, all the so-called 'street children' in Brazil. I want to provide safe places for them so the scum who consider themselves ridding the world of God's children will have to find something better to do with their time.

"Now, I don't really know how to go about it, but after we left from meeting with you and the investigator, I had another idea. I remembered you talking about going to Maryland to see about your friend, the one who is just like a sister to the Donovans."

Karena couldn't believe her ears. Still, she acknowledged her mother's words by adding, "Noelle. Yes, she's involved with one of the Donovan cousins."

Noreen had scooted up in her chair, her brown eyes alight with excitement. "That's right. Well, the name Donovan stuck with me and I did a little research on the computer."

"You were on the computer?" Karena asked.

Noreen looked at her as if she were speaking another language. "Of course, Karena. Everybody does everything on the computer these days. I had to learn or I'd be in the Dark Ages forever."

Again, Karena was shocked silent. She'd had no idea her mother knew how to operate a computer, let alone do Internet research. She figured her mother's free time was filled with housework and tending to her father. How wrong she'd been.

"So anyway, the Donovans have a couple of foundations and they all have specialties. I came across their Children With HIV/AIDS projects and thought about contacting them, you know, for some pointers on getting this type of venture off the ground." Noreen was reaching into her purse and pulling out an envelope. "I've drafted this letter and I want you to take a look at it and tell me what you think."

Karena thought she was dreaming.

Was this really her mother?

She reached for the letter her mother had taken from the envelope and read it. "This is good, Mama. But why don't you just give Beverly Donovan a call. I've met her and her sister-in-law Alma. They do most of the philanthropic work for the family. I could probably even set up a meeting." Beverly Donovan was the mother of the renowned Triple Threat Donovan Brothers, Linc, Adam and Trent. But aside from that, she was a well-respected and well-liked woman in Karena's estimation.

"No," Noreen said adamantly. "I don't want to ride on anybody's coattails. Especially not my daughter's. I'll approach them myself."

"Okay. Then at least let me give you Beverly's home number. It doesn't make sense for you to go through all that red tape trying to get in touch with her when you can just make a phone call." It was Karena's turn to hold up her hand to halt her mother's words. "It's not riding on anybody's coattails, Mama. You're a Lakefield. And while we're not as well-known as the Donovans, we've made our mark in the business and charity arenas. Just call her and tell her your ideas."

Karena was already flipping through her Rolodex. Grabbing a pen, she wrote Beverly Donovan's name, home and business numbers on a Post-it and passed it to her mother.

"I'm just so happy you've found something you want to do after all this time."

Noreen took the paper, stuck it to the corner of her letter and put it and the envelope back in her purse. "You just don't understand. I've had something to do all my life. At different times my responsibilities were different. Now is a new time in my life, a new direction for me."

"I know and I'm happy for you."

Noreen folded her hands in her lap and watched her daughter. "But are you happy, Karena? Are you happy with yourself, with the life you've decided to have? Don't think I don't know how long you've been wanting me to do something different, hating the way I took care of you girls and your father. But that was my decision, my life. What I wanted to do. What about you? Is this what you really want to do with your life?"

"I didn't hate how you took care of us. I just thought you could do so much more."

"I think you can do much more."

Her words made Karena uncomfortable. She shifted in her seat. "I don't know what you mean."

"Yes, you do."

"Mama, this isn't about me. We were talking about you and your new career move." Her mother was the last person she wanted to talk to about Sam or her feelings for Sam.

"You're right," Noreen said with a complacent smile. "But let me tell you something about mothers and housewives, we're very perceptive. I watched you and that investigator, Sam Desdune, at the meeting the other day."

Because she knew what was coming next, Karena sat up and let her elbows rest on her desk. "I met Sam a few months back when I visited Noelle. He's a great guy, a good investigator and a loyal friend. So, yes, we know each other outside of business and this case."

"I'm betting you know each other intimately."

Heat suffused Karena's cheeks, but she prayed the blush wasn't visible. "Mama," she began.

"Don't get all embarrassed, Karena. I've had sex a time or two in my life." Noreen chuckled. "And I still try to get in as much as possible, if truth be told."

Karena closed her eyes momentarily, shaking her head. "Way too much information, Mama."

"I know, I know." Noreen laughed. "But what I was getting at was that you two look like a couple, a very handsome couple, I might add."

Karena sighed. Lying would be foolish.

"We were involved but it didn't work out. Now we're just friends." Were they?

"Was that his decision or yours?"

"It was inevitable," she replied, feeling the painful truth to her words.

"Do you love him?"

"Does it matter?"

For the first time in she couldn't even remember how long, Karena saw Noreen frown.

"Love always matters, Karena. Remember that," she said, standing up and putting her purse on her arm. "Above else, love always matters."

Chapter 25

"You did what?" Lynn set her coffee mug down with a loud clunk as she stared across the table at her younger brother.

Bree shook her head, rolling her eyes. "Please, please, please tell me you didn't."

Breakfast with his sisters was a bad idea, Sam knew it the minute he accepted. But he wasn't doing anything else this Saturday morning, so he'd figured it would be harmless. He should have known better.

It had been a month since he'd seen or heard from Karena, thirty days that he'd thought about her at least three times in each twenty-four-hour interval.

"I just said that either she wanted to give us a chance or she didn't," he tried to backtrack. Bree had been the one to bring Karena up, mentioning that she hadn't called the office and that the invoice for their services had been promptly paid by Lakefield Galleries. Lynn had chimed right in, asking when they were going to meet Karena. So he'd had to tell them where things stood with them and about the last day he'd seen Karena.

"It wasn't like an ultimatum," he continued.

"Then what do you call it?" Lynn asked.

"I call it being honest."

Bree frowned. "I call it being an ass."

Sam had been balling up his napkin and impulsively tossed it at her. "Who asked you?"

Lynn waved a hand between the two of them. "So let me get this straight—she wanted to set guidelines for your relationship, and you wanted the whole nine yards."

"So unyielding," Bree murmured, lifting her cup to her lips to muffle the words.

Ignoring his twin, Sam answered, "Yeah, that sounds about right."

"Did you propose marriage to her?"

"No, I wasn't moving that fast. My point was just that assigning days and times we would spend together was juvenile."

Lynn kept her gaze on Sam, her fingers tapping on the table. "Maybe that's all she could handle right now. Maybe, even though you didn't say marriage, the thought of being totally single and independent one day then shacked up and committed the next was too much, too soon."

"Controlling," Bree said as she finished crunching ice from her finished glass of lemonade. "I told you before you left you were being too controlling, just like Leeza was with you."

Sam cut her an agitated glare. "I told you that was no comparison."

"Are you sure?" Lynn asked. "If memory serves me correctly, you were tired of her making plans for the both of you, accepting invitations, planning how many kids you would have and when, how long you would work and when you would take a break."

His older sister's raised brows had him pausing. Was that what he'd done with Karena?

"I didn't plan anything." He took a deep breath, looking around Lynn's cheery kitchen, then released it. "I didn't tell her any of my plans. I just told her that I needed more than a few days here and there. Was that so wrong?"

"No, but telling her it was your final offer was two points shy of stupid."

Of course this was Bree, and of course he gave her another scathing look. "Since when did you become an expert in the relationship department?"

For a minute she looked bruised by his words, and Sam really did feel like an ass. Bree had gone through a lot with the men in her life, starting with the retired colonel from the Marines who'd stalked and then attacked her earlier this year. She'd had a tug-of-war going on with her current husband before coming to her senses and letting her guard down. Now she seemed happier than Sam had ever seen her.

"I didn't mean it like that," he said quietly.

"I know what you meant, and you're right. I haven't been in enough relationships to give you advice where they're concerned. But I've been a woman all my life and I can tell you there's one thing you never, ever do."

With a nod she looked at Lynn, who nodded back in agreement.

"Never, ever, give a black woman an ultimatum unless you want your pride handed to you on a platter."

Lacing his fingers together, with his elbows propped on the table, Sam dropped his head momentarily. Why did her words sound so true? Why was he slowly realizing how big a mistake he'd made with Karena.

"She's not answering my calls," he said quietly.

"I don't blame her," Bree quipped.

Lynn reached across the table and waited until he extended

his arm to take her hand. "Step back a little from your feelings, from your goals and your wants, and think about her. Think about how you felt when Leeza was railroading your life. Then go see her, don't call, don't write. The best groveling can only be done in person."

When she finished she was smiling, which made Sam smile, too. Like Bree, Lynn hadn't experienced the best of relationships, yet it never seemed as if she'd given up on love. Resigned to her own situation, maybe, but not bitter and cold like some women who'd been scorned could be.

He had a lot to think about, a lot more than he'd been thinking about these past few weeks. Outside of work and brunch with his family, Sam had pretty much stayed in his house, spending time with Romeo and remembering the one night Karena had spent there.

In her hurry to leave she'd left some of her toiletries in his bathroom, a comb on his dresser and a travel-size bottle of aspirin on the nightstand where she'd slept on the left side of his bed.

He hadn't moved any of it, hadn't wanted to disturb the memory in the hopes that it would make her come back.

Tonight, as he walked the shiny wood floors of his home, he gave a lot of thought to what his sisters had said, to what his feelings for Karena were and to how he planned to win her back.

Chapter 26

The wind had turned only slightly chilly as the week before Christmas approached, which was strange for East Coast states, considering this time last year they'd already had two snowstorms.

But Sam wasn't really concerned with the weather. He was more worried about the fact that Karena was still on his mind and still avoiding his calls. He'd be leaving for Trent and Tia's wedding tomorrow morning, going to Las Vegas two days early to attend Trent's bachelor party and other festivities the Donovan family had planned.

The idea of watching another couple take the plunge into matrimonial bliss had him thinking more and more about Karena. His feelings hadn't changed. In fact, they'd only grown stronger in the weeks they'd been separated. Since talking to his sisters, he'd come to terms with the fact that he could have been acting more like Leeza than he cared to admit.

That fact was resonated when he'd had to attend the Fall Ball because his parents weren't able to and his mother thought the family needed a representative. Leeza had immediately clung to him, at which time Sam, once again, had to put her in her place. After that he realized how annoying it had been to have her planning their every move, even before he'd thought about them.

So on some level he could assume Karena had felt that same way. He still wanted her totally committed to him, but he'd seen the advantage to apologizing to her and letting her have a say in their future.

These thoughts and conclusions were what led him to her office this afternoon. He'd received her voice mail one time too many. It was time for a face-to-face.

Astrid wasn't at her desk when he walked through the glass doors, but he didn't mind, he knew the way. Moving purposefully down the hallway, he was startled and annoyed to find her office door open and the room empty.

Where was she?

Going around her desk he noted that her computer was off. There was a desk calendar that he immediately reached for and flipped through, but he didn't see any appointments for today or the days immediately prior. He was just coming around the desk to leave when a decidedly feminine and slightly irritated voice stopped him.

"Well, well, well, what brings you back here?"

Monica Lakefield, dressed in a black business suit that draped her tall frame with a sophisticated air, stood in the doorway.

"Hello, Monica."

"Are we breaking and entering now?" She arched a brow on her perfectly made-up face, folding her arms over her chest and leaning against the doorjamb.

"I'm looking for your sister."

"Really? Which one? I have two, you know."

Try as he might to dislike Karena's older sister, Sam couldn't. After Alex's quick assessment of her, he'd begun thinking how much of a pity it was that a woman as attractive as Monica had decided freezing her emotions forever was better than trying her hand with men again. It was a pity but probably not his battle. He couldn't rescue everybody.

"I've been trying to get in contact with Karena."

"Unsuccessfully, I assume," she quipped. "A fact that only goes to prove my theory of men being a total waste of time."

"That's your theory, huh?" he asked, too intrigued by her words to simply let them go and walk away. "I wonder what could have happened to give you that impression."

Instantly she straightened up, her defenses raised. "I'm just smart enough to spot the bull about twenty minutes before the walking vessels full of testosterone show up."

"Wow, never heard the male species described that way. A little clinical, don't you think?"

Her lips grew to a tight line. "Karena's not here, as you can see. You can leave now."

It was obvious he'd touched a nerve and even more obvious that this particular Lakefield female had a lot of work cut out for the next man who decided to take her on. But Sam was not that man. The Lakefield woman he wanted was playing a game of her own. One he intended to win.

"Where is she?"

"Out of town."

"For how long?"

"None of your business."

Sam exhaled heavily. "Monica, I'm not going to hurt her, if that's what you think you're protecting her from."

"You already did," she replied instantly. "Don't think I'm going to stand by and watch you take another shot at her."

"Karena's a big girl, she can fight her own battles."

"I used to think so until you came along. Then she changed, and I don't know that it's for the better."

"Well, I don't think that's your call."

"She's my sister."

Sam nodded, agreed. "That's not debatable. But she's very important to me."

"Like a business deal or another notch in your bedpost?"

Usually it was the father who posed these questions, guarded his daughter's heart and virtue like this. Dealing with the sister was challenging but not entirely impossible.

"Like a woman whom I'm in love with."

"Bullsh—"

"Monica?" A stern voice came from behind her and had Sam's gaze rising just above Monica's shoulder to meet with Paul Lakefield.

Monica cleared her throat. "Hi, Dad."

"That's not business-appropriate language you were about to use."

"No, it wasn't," she said, casting Sam an irritated gaze. "He's trespassing."

"I don't think so," Paul said, stepping past Monica into Karena's office. "He's looking for Karena, I suspect. And I believe I know why. Leave us alone," he said without even turning to face his daughter again. His tone solicited no argument from Monica as she quickly left the room without another word to Sam.

"Have a seat, son," Paul motioned to Sam.

Going behind Karena's desk again, Sam took a seat in her executive chair while Paul sat in a guest chair. The man looked as if he had a lot on his mind. Sam only hoped it wasn't a lot that involved him.

"Karena's out of town." He began sternly.

"So I heard. Do you know when she'll be back?"

"I'm not really sure. She doesn't talk to me much about things that aren't business-related."

"You sound bothered by that fact."

For a minute it looked as if the older man's shoulders slumped. "I think I am. My daughter and I aren't close."

"I got that impression."

"Did you? Do you know why we aren't close?"

"Not really."

"Because I'm an idiot," he said simply. "Don't look at me like that. I'm not too old or too self-confident to admit my shortcomings."

"I didn't think so," Sam said, trying to keep his voice level so as not to offend.

Paul rubbed his hands down his face and just for a second looked extremely tired. "Raising three daughters isn't easy."

Sam had to chuckle. How many times had his father fretted about something Lynn or Bree did? And now with Bailey in the picture, Lucien seemed to worry just a bit more. Luckily Bailey had stopped working so hard on the Chester case and started spending more time with the family so Lucien could keep a closer eye on her.

"I hope to experience it myself one day."

"You want kids?"

"Yes, I do."

"You want kids with my daughter?"

Blunt. To the point. Accurate. Sam was beginning to like Paul Lakefield.

"Yes, I do."

Paul smiled. "I figured as much. That first day I saw you two together I knew I was about to lose her. It's not a good feeling when a man watches another man take his place in his daughter's life."

"I could never take your place."

"It might be a wise move on your part, son. I don't think

Karena and I related very well. Monica and I are a bit closer because she's the oldest, she's so driven, so cutthroat, like a son would be."

His words touched the alarm bell in Sam's head. "But she's not your son, she's your daughter."

"I know. Scared the hell out of me the moment she was born. I didn't know what to do with a girl. She was so fragile and so sweet, I didn't want to mess her up. So I let Noreen deal with her. Then Karena came along and I knew I was going to lose my mind. Another daughter to protect from the ugliness of the world."

Understanding the meaning behind the man, Sam added, "And then you had Deena."

Paul chuckled. "She was a month premature and has been on the move ever since then. I swear I don't think there's a second in the day that girl slows down. From one thing to another she moves, but she's as happy as can be while she's doing it. It's funny, but I don't worry about her as much. Deena knows exactly what she wants and she's not about to let me, her mother or anybody else stop her."

Paul Lakefield loved his daughters. No matter what the three women may have thought, he loved them, Sam thought, possibly more than he ever would have loved a son.

"Karena's afraid and she doesn't handle fear well." He'd been gazing off somewhere then brought his stare back to Sam. "I think you scare her."

"That wasn't my intention."

Paul shrugged. "Alienating my daughters wasn't mine, either, but it seems I did a pretty good job of it." His lips spread into a smile. "But you've got time to fix it. At least I hope you plan on fixing it."

"That's why I'm here. A wise man once told me that a man can never be too self-confident that he can't admit his shortcomings."

With that Paul's smile grew. He leaned forward in his chair, extended a hand to Sam. "You're a good man, son. A good man for my daughter."

Sam accepted Paul's handshake and his vote of approval. Now if he could only find the woman to tell her.

Chapter 27

Karena was dead tired. She'd spent the past week in Dallas coordinating the move of a new bronze sculpture collection they would be displaying over the holidays at the gallery. It was an impromptu trip scorned by the fact that she missed Sam terribly.

She missed the sound of his voice, the touch of his lips on hers, that eerie way he knew what she was thinking before she even said it. She just missed him. And she thought she might just be the biggest fool in the world for running away from such a perfect man.

Backtrack, rewind—Sam Desdune was not perfect. He was arrogant and bossy and self-serving and compassionate and caring and loyal. He was the man she'd fallen in love with.

Dammit, each time those words filtered through her mind she grew warm inside. Then reality set in and she shivered. Sam was out of her life, he'd given her a choice. She'd chosen and he'd walked. Right or wrong on either part, he was gone.

Emptying her suitcase was a tedious task and one she was not enjoying in the least bit. Her ringing doorbell was a welcome distraction.

"Hey, girl, you finally back in town. I haven't seen you since you stood me up for breakfast weeks ago," Deena said, coming into Karena's apartment like a whirlwind.

The entire time she talked she moved. Pushing past Karena at the door, stripping off her leather jacket and dropping it on the couch, then picking up the television remote and turning it on before plopping down in the center of the living room floor, crossing her legs Indian style.

Used to this entrance, Karena simply closed the door and walked into the living room. "I have chairs, Deena. You're too old to be sitting on the floor like some kindergarten student."

Channels flicked with the speed of light across the television screen as Deena began talking again. "Those chairs look too perfect to sit on. I told you that when you bought them. It's like a showroom in here instead of being a home. Anyway, I didn't come to talk about your furniture."

Still, her words had Karena looking around. She'd liked her furniture when she ordered it out of the catalog. But Deena had a point, it didn't feel like a home. Not like Sam's house did.

"I have some news."

Despite her previous words, Karena found herself dropping to the floor next to her younger sister. "I hope it's good."

"Of course," Deena said, momentarily taking her gaze from the screen and smiling at Karena, who was now right beside her. "You know I was looking for an agent, right? Well, in the meantime I sent my story to a couple of publishers. I didn't really think anybody would like it."

Karena smirked. "Yes, you did. You told me they were going to love it when you wrote the first sentence."

Deena nodded. "That's right, I did. Okay, well one of the publishers did like it and they called me and made me an offer. I took the offer and now my book is going to be published. And the best part is they needed a book to fill their schedule, so my project has been fast-tracked. It'll be released in four months instead of the usual year it takes for a book to go through the publication process."

She would have continued talking if Karena hadn't grabbed her by the shoulders, pulling her close for a big hug. "Oh, Dee! I'm so happy for you. So very, very happy. I told Mama I thought you'd found your niche!"

"Okay, K, you're choking me."

"Oh, sorry," Karena said, releasing her hold but rubbing a hand over her sister's shoulder-length hair and cupping her cheek. "I'm so proud of you, Dee. I'm so very proud of the way you go get what you want despite what anybody says or does. You're such an inspiration."

"What? Wait. Hold on. Has this congratulatory speech just turned to something else? What's up with you, K?"

Tears had already begun to well up in Karena's eyes and she tried to look away. But Deena was fast. She grabbed her by the shoulders and held her still. "What's going on?"

"Nothing," Karena sighed. "Everything and nothing," she added finally.

Deena switched off the television and turned back to Karena. "Start from the beginning and talk slowly so I don't miss anything."

That was funny coming from the woman who talked a mile a minute. But Karena did just that, telling her sister about the first time she'd met Sam in Noelle's kitchen, to the last time she'd seen him on the airstrip at LaGuardia.

"So there, that's my love life in a nutshell." She sighed after a half hour of talking. Reaching up onto the couch, she pulled one of the pillows down, cradled it in her arms and agreed with Deena. This furniture should have been in a showroom, not a living room.

"Hmm, you know what you have to do, right?"

She'd begun rocking back and forth, cradling that hard-ass pillow as if it were a life preserver keeping her from drowning in self-pity. "No. What?"

"You have to go get your man," Deena said as if it were as apparent as the sun setting outside.

"The man gave me an ultimatum, Dee. Why would I want to be with someone like that? What if he thinks that's how to get his way with me all the time? I can't keep giving in. I'll lose myself if I do."

"You lost yourself a long time ago, girl."

"What?"

"The minute you decided Mama needed to do something better with herself you embarked on a crusade to save Noreen Lakefield instead of to be Karena Lakefield. I saw it and figured you and Monica both had a few lessons to learn. So I kept my younger-sister mouth shut. But now you're in trouble so I'm going to lay it on the line. Stop using Mama as an excuse. She's not the reason you're afraid to fall in love and commit to a man."

"Wait a minute. I don't think you know what you're talking about."

"None of you ever do. But I see and hear a lot of stuff being the youngest in this family. I see that Daddy doesn't know how to communicate with us even though he loves us. The females in his life have just completely thrown him for a loop. I see that Mama is finally coming into her own, on her own terms, in her own time. But then I knew she'd get there. That's why I never harassed her the way you did. I see that Monica is going to self-implode if she doesn't get off her high horse soon. And I see that you are on the precipice of either moving forward with your own life, or getting stuck in the same type of rut—despite your warnings to Mama—that you assumed she was in all these years."

Karena could only blink. Deena had said a mouthful, nothing unusual. But her words made sense, her insights were right on target. And she was the baby of the family.

"I...I don't know...what to say."

"That's funny, you and Mama are usually the ones who do know what to say to me." Deena chuckled, her deep dimples adding a light to her smile that was hers alone.

"Anyway, as I was saying before, you need to go get your man. It's obvious he loves you or he wouldn't have wasted his time with the ultimatum. And it's obvious you love him or you wouldn't be sitting on this floor whining about the nerve he had to talk to you that way. So I say you pack your bag and head straight to his house."

"I can't move in with him, Deena. I need my own space."

"So don't move in with him. Yet. But drop those guidelines you proposed. There are no guidelines to falling in love."

"How do you know? You've never been in love."

"Didn't I just sell a romance novel? Girl, please. I wrote one hell of a love story. I know what I'm talking about."

Karena couldn't help but laugh, but in the next hour she listened attentively to her romance-author baby sister's advice on how she should fix her relationship with Sam.

Unfortunately she couldn't take Deena's advice. Trent and Tia's wedding was later today.

Chapter 28

The Mt. Charleston Resort was a sophisticated, yet quaint, venue. Of course, the Donovans had rented the entire resort to accommodate Trent and Tia's wedding.

Karena had checked into the room she would be staying in tonight with just enough time to shower and change into the dress she was wearing to the wedding. The late arrival was due to the indecision that had plagued her in the weeks since receiving the invitation.

It had come one week to the day she'd walked out of Sam Desdune's life, for good. It wasn't that she didn't love him. That cruel twist of fate was alive and breathing each day she awoke. The more pertinent issue had been if she could live up to what he expected of her. But after talking to Deena and doing some heavy soul-searching on the plane, Karena had decided that it wasn't about being what people expected you to be, but about remaining true to herself. She couldn't be what her father wanted, or what she thought he wanted. She could only be her. And she couldn't base her life's goals on her mother's choices. She had to find her own happiness.

But what could she do to be happy?

Each time she asked that question, Sam's face had ultimately appeared in her mind's eye. Unfortunately, now, after leaving the upbeat and always-optimistic aura of Deena Lakefield, she thought that ship had possibly sailed. Sam wanted a woman who was sure of herself and ready for the commitment he offered, and that's what he deserved.

So why was she here? In Las Vegas at the wedding she was sure he would also be at. Her invitation had stemmed from her relationship with Noelle and the fact that her mother had, in her own lifestyle change, contacted Beverly Donovan to discuss their families joining together in a philanthropic endeavor. Sam's, however, would come from the fact that he was as close to Trent Donovan as family and they were business partners. There was no doubt in her mind he was here. All the doubt rested on whether she could handle seeing him again.

She passed a huge elegantly decorated ballroom as hostesses garbed in chocolate-brown gowns and matching bolero jackets guided guests to the Canyon Terrace, where the wedding would take place. It was Christmas Eve and still a very comfortable fifty-six degrees in Vegas, so an outdoor ceremony wasn't as strange as she'd originally thought upon arriving.

Rows of white chairs occupied two sides of the terrace while a rose-petal-filled runner stretched down the center to stop at an arch loaded with cream-and-beige-colored flowers. The seats were just about full, since it was only ten minutes until five o'clock and the wedding was slated to start promptly at five. Hurriedly Karena slipped into one of the back rows, taking a seat at the far end.

Only a few minutes after she'd sat music began to play. It was an instrumental version of an old classic, "Ribbon In The Sky" by Stevie Wonder.

Henry and Beverly Donovan stepped out onto the terrace pushing a double stroller. Several guests oohed and aahed at Linc and Jade's twins, Torian and Tamala. Almost eight months old now, the two little girls were the epitome of little princesses with their frilly pink hats and satin dresses.

A tall woman with beautiful blue-gray hair pulled back into a neat chignon stepped onto the runner next. She, too, pushed a stroller. This one was a dark brown, decorated with beige lace. The baby inside could not be easily seen. So just like several of the other guests, Karena found herself lifting slightly out of her seat to get a glance.

Trent and Tia had welcomed a baby boy to the Donovan clan just one week before Thanksgiving. Immediately after the birth, Tia had set her final wedding plans in motion, Noelle had informed her. Trevor Donovan had his father wrapped tightly around his finger already.

Speak of the devil, Trent Donovan eased onto the terrace without his normally brooding stare. Today, he looked handsome as ever dressed in a tuxedo the color of buttermilk, a silk tie that matched the chocolate color of the hostesses' gowns and a brown calla lily boutonniere on his lapel. He even cracked a small smile as his younger brother, Adam, stepped beside him wearing a dark brown tuxedo and the two of them began walking down the aisle.

Next came the bridal party. Noelle was escorted by Maxwell Donovan, Trent's cousin. She looked great, her strapless mocha-hued dress hugging her upper body then flaring out with a gathered skirt. Karena smiled because in addition to her outer beauty there was a glow about Noelle as she moved down the aisle, an aura of happiness that seemed to float along with her. Karena was jealous but inhaled deeply and focused on the reason why she was here instead of the mistakes she'd made in the past.

Wearing the same dress as Noelle, Jade Donovan was escorted by her husband, Linc. They looked so domestic and so right together.

Two of the cutest little girls she'd ever seen followed, tossing more flowers onto the runner minutes before Camille Davis Donovan made her entrance. She was elegant in her dress that mimicked Jade and Noelle's perfectly except for the deep chocolate-brown color.

Then the music changed to another instrumental tune, "A Whole New World" by Regina Belle and Peabo Bryson. The minister lifted his hands for everyone to stand and Karena's heart pitter-pattered in her chest as a beautiful Tia St. Claire stepped onto the runner with her father holding her shaking hand. Slowly they moved down the aisle, just as slowly, almost as if with each step, Karena's heart broke a fraction more.

As the ceremony proceeded Karena listened intently, watching as Tia and Trent pledged their love to each other and then kissed to seal their union. After being pronounced and before walking back up the aisle as was customary, Trent went to the silver-haired woman and retrieved the stroller she'd pushed in. Coming back up the aisle now were Tia, Trent and little Trevor Donovan.

A family.

Watching them was like a newsflash.

Karena knew exactly what she wanted to make herself happy.

He'd seen her the moment she stood to exit the terrace, following the rest of the guests into the ballroom where the reception would be held.

He'd thought about her every second since he'd left her father in her office.

Now, as he made his way to the table where she was sitting alone, for the first time he knew in forever, his heart hammered. His palms began to sweat slightly as nervousness about approaching a woman began to set in.

It was foolish. He'd already met her, slept with her, confessed his love to her. He shouldn't be nervous about sitting down beside her and saying hello. Yet when he came to the table, pulled out the chair and sat down, all words fled from his mind.

She turned to him, her gaze instantly grabbing his, and she didn't speak. Instead she cupped his face in her hands, pulled him to her and kissed him, soundly, assuredly, passionately.

"Are you ready?" she asked the minute their lips separated.

"Ready for what?" Sam asked, his voice shaking just slightly. He hadn't known what to expect when he'd sat down beside her. That kiss wasn't it. And the heated gaze she was giving him wasn't it, either. But he wasn't about to complain.

"For me."

Questions were pointless. The reception was quickly forgotten as Sam stood, pushed his chair back and reached for her hand.

"Let's go."

Without a word Karena put her hand in his and followed him out of the ballroom, down the hall to the set of elevators that led up to the rooms.

Sam's stride was quick, his finger jabbing insistently over the button signaling the elevator. They entered the small space, standing all the way to the back against the wall. When the doors closed his arms went around her waist and she felt herself being pulled against the impenetrable strength of his chest. His lips came down quick and hot against hers. His tongue stroking, begging, promising what was to come.

Her knees buckled and she leaned in to him. Her arms twined around his neck, running over the smooth, close cut of his hair. This was what she wanted, Karena thought as her mind spun out of control, every bone in her body weakening with his touch, with his kiss. Their tongues clashed and dueled for control.

One minute she leaned against his chest enfolded in strong arms and the next her back was against the wall, his large hands gripping her bottom tightly. Ripples of pleasure soared through her at a rapid pace.

His hot mouth was everywhere. From her mouth, to her cheek, to her ear, down her neck… He devoured her and she melted in his arms.

Ting. The elevator came to a smooth halt. Not that she noticed it. Luckily Sam had. A ragged moan sounded and he reluctantly pulled away.

Karena opened her eyes. Her vision blurred with passion. "Your room or mine?"

"Whichever is closest," was his reply.

Stepping off the elevator, she dug in her purse and found her key card. She was 221. Simultaneously Sam had reached into his back pocket, retrieving his key card. He was 204.

Showing their cards to each other, Sam grinned, grabbed her by the hand and headed toward room 204.

Mt. Charleston was a great resort, with wonderful views and four-star rooms. But that was the farthest thing from Karena's mind at this very moment.

They should talk, she knew. She had things to say, things to clear up, but the moment Sam closed that door behind them and took her in his arms, all those thoughts slipped away.

His hands moved like lightning, ridding her of every piece

of clothing she wore. Hers moved just as frantically until they both stood naked. While she thought they'd make their way back to the bedroom, Sam had other ideas.

He kissed her again, his tongue moving wildly over hers. She gasped for air, trying to keep up with his hands, his moans.

"Sam." His name broke free from her lips as he backed her to a wall.

"Shhh, baby. I've got this."

His words were arrogant, controlling, demanding as he turned her so that she was facing the wall and he was close behind her. They should have bothered her, but the feel of his rigid arousal tapping persistently against her bottom replaced any agitation with desire so strong and hot she whimpered with its impact.

Her head fell back, resting against his shoulder, her hands reaching back to skim the sides of his thighs moving high to cup his tight buttocks. She was shaking, anxiously awaiting his entrance.

Strong hands palmed her breasts, lifting the heavy mounds and squeezing until her puckered nipples rolled through the tips of his fingers.

She gasped, licked her lips and moaned.

He bit her lobe then flicked the tingling skin with the tip of his tongue. Her heart pounded in anticipation. Her lids, heavy with arousal, closed of their own accord.

The flat of his tongue traced a long hot trail from her neck down to her collarbone while he bent his knees, encouraging her to do the same.

She was open, her essence rolling down her thighs, her scent permeating the air. Abandoning her breasts, his hands spread her legs wider, gripping her inner thighs.

She bit her bottom lip until she thought she might

draw blood. She was so hot for him, so ready for total satisfaction.

Sliding both hands farther up her thighs, he used his thumbs to spread her nether lips, his fingers eagerly slipping along the heated flesh. He dipped his knees lower and she followed suit, reveling in his thick length moving enticingly against her buttocks. He slipped one finger into her opening as the other hand grasped the bud of her arousal and squeezed. Coherent thought long since a thing of the past, she hissed, cursed and then begged him for more.

"I love you, Karena," he whispered as the tip of his manhood breached her opening.

Her palms flattened on the wall as she took him inside. That wasn't all she was taking in. His words resonated in her ears, swirling around inside to mingle with the desire that only Sam could incite. It was now or never, she knew. She had thought this situation through until her mind was about to explode, only to find the answer was so simple: love always mattered.

"I love you, too, Sam."

Like music to his ears her words touched him, wrapping around his heart with silken fingers. He thrust his hips, planting himself deeper inside, wanting to be one with her and only her.

For endless moments there was nothing else, only the movement of their bodies, the joining of their passion, the fusion of their hearts.

Pulling out of her, Sam lifted Karena into his arms, carried her into the bedroom and lay her on the bed.

"I'm sorry, baby," he said, coming to lay beside her.

She rolled to her side and cupped his face in her hands. "No, I'm sorry. Guidelines were stupid."

"And pushing you into something you weren't ready for was stupider."

Sam pulled her close and she wrapped her arms around his waist.

"We're some couple, huh?" she whispered as he lifted her leg and dropped it over his hips, maneuvering himself so that he was slipping slowly inside her heated moistness once more.

"We're a perfect couple," he said, his lips finding hers, taking her for another ride on desire's train.

Perfect was an understatement as they moved in sync with one another, peaking and cresting at the same time, whispering words of love and contentment until they both fell asleep.

Epilogue

Karena was coming for dinner and to spend the weekend, Sam hoped. He hadn't asked her to specifically. That was part of their taking-things-as-they-came agreement.

There were no set days that they met. He awakened in the morning, went to work and either called or e-mailed her. She did the same. Sometime during the course of the day, one of them would mention getting together and it would be. A few nights he'd stayed at her condo, but more nights she'd stayed with him, in his house, with his dog.

She loved Romeo almost as much as Sam did, and for a moment Sam had been jealous. But when she'd expressed how much she'd wanted a dog of her own while growing up, he'd understood completely. And Romeo, big spoiled baby that he was, accepted all of Karena's affection while still demanding time from Sam.

So as he lit candles throughout the living room, Sam hummed an old Keith Sweat song, "Make It Last Forever," knowing that no matter what, Karena was his forever.

She pulled up into his driveway, turned off the ignition and drummed her fingers on the steering wheel once more. The decision was final. It was impetuous and insane and totally out of character for her. Yet it felt absolutely right.

There was no denying how she felt when she was with Sam. Just as there was no ignoring the decrease in her headaches and increase in her appetite since they'd begun seeing each other. She felt healthier, more energized since she'd begun leaving business at the gallery except when absolutely necessary—and keeping Monica's demands and opinions to a minimum.

She hadn't discussed this decision with anyone. Hadn't wanted any outside opinions or interference. This was her life, her moment, her happiness.

Stepping out of the car, she went to the trunk and popped it open. She was just reaching in to get her suitcase when she heard Romeo's familiar bark. Turning quickly, she braced herself for his greeting.

He jumped up and she caught him, his full length towering over hers. Turning her face, she caught his lapping tongue with her cheek. "Hey, boy. Hey. You miss me?"

"We missed you," Sam said, making a silent approach. "Down, Romeo," he ordered the dog.

Romeo, albeit reluctantly, obeyed and rested at Karena's side. She was petting his head when she looked up to see Sam, but something else caught her gaze.

On a leash Sam held tightly in his hands was a black Great Dane with natural ears. Its eyes were darker than Romeo's, more subtle, just a tad more relaxed.

"I figured since I had a girl now, Romeo needed one, too,"

Sam said, shrugging, releasing the leash a little and offering it to her.

"She's beautiful. Isn't she, Romeo?" Beside her, Romeo stood. Sam gave him a stern look and he remained still.

The girl beside him, however, had already begun to move, lolling her head, extending her neck as she reached for Romeo or Karena, or both of them.

"What's her name?" Karena asked, taking a tentative step forward and falling to her knees to get a closer look. As she'd hoped, the girl ducked her head and fell right into Karena's caress. Her heart soared.

"Juliet."

Karena's head snapped up as she looked at Sam, who was smiling down at her.

"Yeah, she's yours."

"Mine?" Karena whispered.

"All yours."

Karena moved so quickly jumping into Sam's arms that he released Juliet's leash and the dog took off running. Romeo followed suit and Sam laughed, hugging Karena tightly and spinning her around.

"You said you always wanted a dog."

She was nodding as he stopped spinning and put her down. Tears filled her eyes as she looked up at him. "I did. I really did want a dog."

"And now you've got one," he said, using the pad of his thumb to swipe at the tear falling from her eyes.

"I've got two," she said, smiling. "Romeo and Juliet. Perfect."

Sam lowered his head, kissing her lightly. When he pulled his lips away, she whispered, "Why don't you help me take my bags inside and then we can finish this?"

"Your bags?" he asked quizzically.

"Yeah," she said, smiling and nodding toward the trunk

of her car that was still open. "My bags. There are too many for me to carry alone."

He looked over her shoulder, saw the trunk full of suitcases. "Ah, baby, how long are you planning to stay?"

"How does forever sound?"

She was in his arms again, spinning in another circle of love. "It sounds damned good. Damned perfect."

* * * * *